A STOLEN KISS

"Do you want to marry him?" Christopher asked. "Of course, you do," he said, scornfully answering his own question. "Lord Whitby is what you and all the silly little debutantes want."

"You know nothing about me!" Cassandra shouted.

He grasped her shoulders and Cassandra turned her face away from him. "I can't let you do it, Cassandra!" he declared and crushed her slim body against his chest.

Cassandra's head was spinning. Maybe Lord Whitby had been right. Maybe she had drunk too much champagne, after all.

Her heart was beating so hard and fast that she feared it would leap from her chest altogether. But that was all right because, incredibly, through her thin gown and fine muslin chemise pressed so close to Christopher's chest, she could feel his heart beating just as fast as hers.

It didn't occur to her to fight *him* off.

The look in his wonderful hazel eyes was so compelling that she had no choice but to raise her face and watch those eyes catch fire as he covered her mouth with his.

She tasted hunger and champagne and something fruity like strawberries.

Delicious . . .

Books by Kate Huntington

THE CAPTAIN'S COURTSHIP

THE LIEUTENANT'S LADY

LADY DIANA'S DARLINGS

MISTLETOE MAYHEM

A ROGUE FOR CHRISTMAS

THE MERCHANT PRINCE

TOWN BRONZE

Published by Zebra Books

TOWN BRONZE

Kate Huntington

ZEBRA BOOKS
KENSINGTON PUBLISHING CORP.
http://www.kensingtonbooks.com

ZEBRA BOOKS are published by

Kensington Publishing Corp.
850 Third Avenue
New York, NY 10022

All Kensington titles, imprints and distributed lines are available at special quantity discounts for bulk purchases for sales promotion, premiums, fund-raising, educational or institutional use.

Special book excerpts or customized printings can also be created to fit specific needs. For details, write or phone the office of the Kensington Special Sales Manager: Kensington Publishing Corp., 850 Third Avenue, New York, NY 10022. Attn. Special Sales Department. Phone: 1-800-221-2647.

Zebra and the Z logo Reg. U.S. Pat. & TM Off.

First Printing: February 2003
10 9 8 7 6 5 4 3 2

Printed in the United States of America

This book is dedicated to Aunt Carolyn and Uncle Dave Ruppert, Aunt Marilyn Gnau, Uncle Bill and Aunt Mary Helen Saluke, Uncle Don and Aunt Ann Saluke, Aunt Marge and Uncle Max Yoos, and in memory of Aunt Alice Hoch, Uncle Bob Saluke, and Uncle Francis Gnau.

You've loved me, taught me, and laughed with me. Thank you for enriching my life.

One

Christopher Warrender opened one eye and gave a wolfish smile when the man of business sent to Dover to accompany him to his grandfather's country estate cowered in the opposite seat of the coach and surreptitiously pulled a handkerchief over his nose.

The poor fellow looked fit to cast up his accounts, and Christopher did not blame him in the least.

He knew he stank to high heaven. Anyone would after spending eleven years in the dankest of prisons the bloody frogs had to offer.

Bitche, Valenciennes, Besançon—Christopher had been a reluctant guest of them all courtesy of the former Emperor of France after he had taken into custody all the English travelers who arrived on French shores in 1803. These optimistic worthies eager to sample the pleasures of Paris had left England during the so-called Peace of Amiens, only to find upon landing at Calais that negotiations had broken down and they were now hostages of the French government. Christopher, a callow youth of eighteen at the time, had come to Europe with his tutor at his grandfather's command, for Jasper Warrender, Viscount Adderly, believed that no man was truly educated until he had first toured the major cities of the polite world and mixed with continental society.

Thanks to his grandfather, Christopher certainly *had* received an education!

He now knew how to fight, how to pick locks, and how to speak gutter French like a native.

Christopher was well aware that, had he behaved himself, he could have stayed the whole eleven years in comparative comfort in Verdun, the city where the English hostages of quality continued to have balls and routs and dine on delicacies provided by rapacious merchants for a price, just as if they had never left England.

But Christopher, ungrateful for these concessions to his noble birth, had persisted in distressing a series of wardens by beating up his guards and trying to escape. He had almost made it to the harbor once after traveling cross-country dressed in rags and pretending to be a farmer.

He was, in fact, planning another escape when he was unexpectedly released from prison and found himself on his way home.

To Devonshire.

It was more frightening, in some ways, than the notorious Fortress of Bitche. At least *there* he had known what to expect. Now that all his concentration was no longer focused on escape, he found himself oddly bereft of purpose.

The fields and cottages they passed looked just the same. He might never have left. He opened the windows just to breathe the air of rural England. This is what he had risked his life for, over and over, as a hostage.

Still, when the journey from the coast was over, it was with some trepidation that he entered the house where he had been born. How many of the souls that had inhabited his youth were still alive?

"Mr. Christopher," Sims, his grandfather's old butler, cried joyfully as he threw his arms around Christopher. For the first time in many years Christopher felt his eyes mist over with tears, which he quickly hid. Had Sims somehow shrunk? The top of his bald head came to the middle of Christopher's chest. Then the butler stepped back and looked shamefacedly at the floor. "Forgive me, sir. I don't know what came over me."

Christopher grinned.

"It is good to see you, too, Sims," he said. His own voice seemed rusty from disuse.

"I shall inform my lord of your arrival at once," the butler said in a more decorous tone. He wrinkled his stately nose. "And order a bath."

"Perhaps I should have the bath first," Christopher said ruefully. He couldn't face his grandfather like this! "No need to disturb his lordship. I'll just go along to my room, shall I, and see him in the—"

"Christopher, my boy!" cried a hearty voice that Christopher would know anywhere.

Too late.

Christopher turned to face his grandfather, that stiff-rumped old tyrant who had bullied him throughout his childhood and adolescence in his zeal to groom him for the onerous task of stepping into his shoes when he stuck his spoon in the wall.

The smile faded from the viscount's face as his shrewd eyes took in Christopher's shaggy, unkempt hair, unshaven face, and ragged clothes. As he approached, Christopher could see the exact moment he got within range of his prison stench by the way his eyes widened.

"You . . . have changed," the viscount said.

"You have not changed at all, Grandfather," Christopher replied, and meant it.

"You are taller," the old man said speculatively. "And you have lost your youthful chubbiness."

"Prison food has that effect on a man," Christopher said grimly.

"With your hair cut properly, and your face shaved, you will be quite presentable," the old man said.

"You relieve my mind," Christopher said, lifting one eyebrow.

The viscount apparently took this remark at face value. He merely nodded, when such sarcasm would have earned Christopher a sharp scold in his youth.

"Fortunately, Cassandra went to bed hours ago with a headache," the old man continued. "It would not do for her to see you like this."

"Cassandra! You mean she's still here?"

"Of course she is," the viscount said. "The girl is my ward. Where else would she be?"

"I assumed she would be married by now."

"It is not *my* fault she has failed to find a husband," he said defensively. "I have been sending her regularly to the subscription balls. The girl is too headstrong and too picky by half! She insists that nothing will do for her but a grand London Season and a husband who is a very pink of the *ton,* for she refuses to shackle herself to any of the jumped-up country squires in this neighborhood."

"She hasn't changed, then," Christopher said glumly. When he last saw the Honorable Miss Cassandra Davies, she had been a bossy, imperious little brat of eleven, who had no compunction about telling Christopher that she had no intention of marrying a fat, spotty, spineless podge like him, even if her guardian locked her in the cellar with the rats and fed her bread and water for a year.

The feeling was entirely mutual.

The knowledge that Cassandra was willing to take her chances with the rats rather than marry him had been a profound relief until Christopher realized his grandfather was prepared to do that very thing to get the richly dowered heiress shackled to his heir. If the war hadn't resumed and Napoleon taken Christopher and his fellow travelers into custody, he no doubt would have found himself married to Cassandra as soon as he set foot back on English soil.

When looked at this way, his eleven years of imprisonment in a series of unspeakable French prisons seemed almost a blessing.

"Cassandra has grown into a vastly pretty girl," the viscount was saying with a matchmaker's gleam in his eye. "I am sure you will be pleased when you see her."

Not bloody likely, Christopher thought.

"I would like to go to my room now," he said instead.

"Of course, of course," the viscount said. "You will need rest after your long journey."

"Yes. Good night, then, Grandfather."

His grandfather surprised him very much by grasping his hand. The thin but still strong fingers closed convulsively on Christopher's as if he were reluctant to let him go.

"I thought you dead," the old man said. To Christopher's surprise, his grandfather's voice cracked on the words.

"I thought the same of you," Christopher admitted, "when you did not pay the ransom."

"I made inquiries through official channels, and I was told you and your tutor both had died at Verdun. I received no ransom demand."

"Mr. Gardiner did die. I hope you notified his family."

"Yes," the viscount said. "Of course. We even had a memorial service for you in the chapel. Everyone in the neighborhood attended. You must believe me, boy. If I had known you were still alive, I would have moved heaven and earth to get you home."

"I do believe you," Christopher said.

He had no illusions that the old man harbored much affection for the unsatisfactory lump that was his heir. However, Christopher was the only surviving descendent of the Warrender male line, and, therefore, the old man's only hope of leaving his legacy to posterity.

Tomorrow after his first night's sleep between clean sheets in eleven years would be soon enough to tell the old man that he wouldn't marry the Honorable Miss Cassandra Davies if the skinny little witch were the last female left on earth!

Cassandra Davies defiantly took a sip of the scalding tea and stared out onto the extensive gardens of her jailer's vast estate. Some might have thought the gardens pretty, and they were. But the roses had been in bloom for some time, and their slightly browned edges and sweet, heavy perfume, while not unpleasant, indicated something perilously close to the beginning stages of rot.

Like herself.

At twenty-two, she still was considered a young woman. But two years beyond that, her bloom would be off. She had been nowhere and seen nothing except her guardian's house.

Now, with the return seemingly from the dead of Christopher Warrender, it appeared that she would be buried here if she didn't nip *that* nonsense in the bud!

This was why she had insisted that her breakfast be brought to her here, on the terrace. She had no wish to encounter her guardian's precious grandson over the teacups.

In fact, she had no wish to see him at all.

While not precisely sorry that the official notification of his death had been untrue, Cassie found the heir's survival vastly inconvenient. After spurning every single one of the April squires who had courted her over the years, she almost had the old man talked into taking her to London to find a husband.

Leave it to fat, spotty Kit Warrender to spoil sport!

Seething, she took another sip of the tea, not caring that it burned her tongue. And the sweet biscuits were as ashes in her mouth. In disgust, she pushed the plate away and stared out over the roses.

Nothing ever happened to her here; nothing ever would.

One day followed the other in humdrum monotony.

She awoke. She dressed. She ate. She rode. She met with the housekeeper. She sketched or embroidered. She paid calls or received calls. She ate. She read or played the pianoforte. She went to bed. The next day she awoke. She dressed. She ate. . . .

No excitement. No surprises. No expectation that anything would ever change.

She had been waiting the whole of her twenty-two years for something to happen, but nothing ever did.

She had just lifted her cup to her lips again when a brown head of hair popped into her line of vision from the garden. The wide, hazel eyes showed white all around, the nostrils quivered, and the apparition had the leaf of some green plant clenched in its teeth.

Cassandra screamed and jumped to her feet, clutching her throat with a convulsive hand.

"Who are you?" she cried out. "What are you doing there, spying on me? And what is that thing in your mouth?"

The man stood to his full height and stared at her. He took the leaf from his mouth, took a bite and chewed.

"Spinach," he said after a moment. "There was no breakfast laid out yet, and I was hungry."

Now that she got a good look at him, she was even more alarmed.

He was tall and thin, although his shoulders were broad. His unkempt long hair was dark brown, and damp around the ends. He was in undress—pantaloons and big bare feet, and his shirt was open halfway down his lightly furred chest. The shirt's flowing sleeves had little patches of dirt and grass stain on them. His face was all too familiar, although the well-defined, bladelike cheekbones had been lost in spotty, chubby cheeks the last time she saw him.

She hadn't seen eyes of that precise shade of mingled green and amber for eleven years, but she would have known them anywhere.

"Christopher Warrender!" she exclaimed in disgust. She put her hands on her hips. "What are you doing out here in the garden, scaring me to death!"

He didn't answer.

Instead, he leapt over the wrought-iron railing that separated the terrace from the gardens in a graceful motion and stared like a starving man at the teapot.

"May I have some?" he asked.

Cassandra sighed.

"I only have the one cup."

"This one will do," he said.

"Why are you shaking like that? Are you ill?"

"No," he said. He took her empty cup and held it

out to her. With a snort of annoyance, she poured tea in it and watched his Adam's apple bob as he drank it straight down.

"More," he said when he was finished. She obliged.

When he finished, he wiped his mouth and looked at the biscuits.

"Oh, go ahead," she snapped.

He gave her a beatific smile, sat down on the decorative little wrought-iron chair, pulled the plate close, and broke the first biscuit in two. He examined the broken pieces carefully.

"What are you doing?" she asked.

"Looking for weevils," he said matter-of-factly.

"That's disgusting!"

"Only if you find some," he told her. She narrowed her eyes, trying to decide whether he was joking. "These look safe enough."

Now that he apparently had determined the biscuits were uninhabited, he ate them quickly and messily, even the one from which she had taken a bite.

"Good," he said, looking at the table as if for more.

"If you're hungry, you can simply order the servants to bring food to you," she said in exasperation. "You are the heir. They have to bring you anything you ask for."

He merely looked at her as if this had never occurred to him.

"Never mind. I'll take care of it," she said. She went to the door that led to the house and spoke to a young woman wearing an apron and a white cap.

"I am not going to marry you, you know," Cassandra said when she returned to him. "Even if you *have* lost your wits and your grandfather needs a woman to take care of you."

He cocked one eyebrow at her.

"Did I ask?"

"No, you don't have to." Cassandra started pacing. "I know how his mind works. If we're not careful, we'll be married before the cat can lick her ear."

He started to answer her, but she gave him a sign to be still. They could not very well discuss this in front of the servants, and three of them were stepping onto the terrace now with covered dishes in their hands.

They removed the teapot, cup, and empty biscuit plate to set down a dish of eggs, one of kippers, and one of bacon. A maidservant followed with a tray containing a fresh pot of tea, two more cups, two clean plates, silver utensils, a plate of toast, and another plate of biscuits. When the maidservant had arranged the table to her satisfaction, Cassandra nodded dismissal.

Her childhood nemesis looked at her with speechless gratitude, then he began piling his plate with food, watching her all the while as if he feared she would reconsider and take it all away from him.

His lower lip trembled as he took his first bite of kipper. His eyes filled with tears.

Oh, merciful heavens.

"Stop that at once," she hissed. "You can't cry *here*! Pull yourself together, for pity's sake!"

"Are you quite sure," he said wistfully, "that you won't marry me after all?"

Christopher could have bitten his tongue once the words were out of his mouth, but the kippers were so wonderful, *she* was so wonderful, he could not help himself.

Cassandra Davies, indeed, had grown into a vastly pretty girl. She was dressed in a charming, high-waisted gown that had little lavender flowers with tiny green leaves printed all over it. Her straight, ash blond hair was confined with a lavender ribbon. Her melting blue eyes were sheer perfection.

Then she had to open those soft pink lips and ruin it all.

"Not if you were the last man on earth!" she sputtered.

Same old Cassie.

Of course, Christopher had to admit few women would be eager to marry a man prone to discuss weevils over the breakfast cups.

He was about to tell her he had been joking to save face, but she regarded him with an expression so earnest that he couldn't get the words out of his mouth.

"Christopher," she said gently, "you do *not* want to marry me."

"But I—"

She put her hand over his. It was so soft and white. He curled his fingers so she could not see his dirty, jagged nails. She smelled like flowers, and he drew back a little for fear she could still smell the prison stench on his person, even though he had scrubbed and scrubbed every inch of his skin last night in the steaming hip bath of water the servants had brought to him before he went to bed.

"You have not seen an Englishwoman for years, so I probably look good to you," she said, "but I'm not. Trust me. I would make you a *very* bad wife. I would dedicate my *life* to making you a very bad wife."

"You would?"

"Yes. Because if I have to marry you, please believe I will be miserable, and I would make *you* miserable, too. I couldn't help myself."

He couldn't think of a word to say to this.

"If Lord Adderly hadn't received word of your release from France, I would be in London now, enjoying my first Season," she said bitterly. "Now I'll probably never get away from here."

"I'm terribly sorry to ruin your plans by failing to expire at a time convenient to you," he said dryly.

"No, no!" she said, sounding conscience-stricken. "That *did* sound horrid. Of course, I'm not sorry you are not dead. It just makes things . . . difficult."

Before he could assure her that nothing short of a loaded pistol would get him anywhere near the altar with her, his grandfather came out onto the terrace, wreathed in smiles.

"There you are, you naughty children," he said, wagging his finger at them. "Having breakfast on the terrace without a chaperon."

Christopher rose to his feet at once and hastily wiped his greasy lips with a napkin. Cassandra's face colored delicately, but Christopher could tell it was more from anger than embarrassment.

"It isn't what it looks like," she snapped. "I found him foraging in the garden for food and ordered the servants to bring him breakfast."

"Foraging for food?" the viscount said, looking at Christopher as if he had two heads. "And, sir, you are improperly dressed. You cannot have breakfast with a young lady without your *coat*!"

"Sorry, sir," Christopher muttered.

"Don't shout at him," Cassandra said, moving protectively in front of Christopher. "You'll only make him nervous." She lowered her voice. "Can't you see the poor thing isn't himself?"

"Nonsense! All he needs is marriage to a good woman," the old man blustered.

"There! Did you hear that?" Cassandra shrieked. "No! Absolutely not! I am sorry as I can be for the poor creature, but I simply cannot marry . . . that."

She indicated Christopher—his shaggy hair, his unkempt hands, his grass-stained shirt—with a helpless gesture of her graceful hands.

"You go too far, miss!" the old man roared. "Christopher is my grandson, and more than a match for you in blood! Your father wanted this match for you, girl, and so do I. I shall have the banns proclaimed this Sunday."

"Over my dead body!" Cassandra said defiantly.

"If need be," her guardian said with a smile that showed all his teeth.

Christopher backed away from them and covered his mouth with both hands. His eyes filled with tears. He could not restrain a strange snorting sound from escaping.

"*Now* look what you've done!" Cassandra said to the viscount. She put a slender arm around Christopher's shoulders. "You've frightened him. There, there, Christopher. He doesn't mean it."

She thought he was weeping, when he was only trying to keep from laughing into their affronted faces. Was ever a situation so absurd?

He made a noncommittal sound and, bending over slightly, turned his face into Cassandra's shoulder. He couldn't resist all that sweet, fragrant softness. She jumped away from him as if she had been scalded.

"I bloody well *do* mean it!" the enraged viscount shouted. "You *will* marry Christopher."

"No," Christopher said. This had gone far enough.

"I beg your pardon?" the old man demanded in disbelief.

"No," Christopher repeated. "I am not going to marry Cassandra. I am not going to marry *anybody*, at least not right away. I didn't spend eleven years in prison so that you could make me marry the first pretty girl I see."

"Now see here, you young jackanapes—" the viscount began.

"I'd like to look about me first," Christopher said right over him. "See if there's anyone around who suits me better. In London."

"London?" the viscount and Cassandra repeated at the same time.

"Good for you," Cassandra said approvingly.

"You be quiet, missy," the old man shouted. "As for you, sir," he added to Christopher with a forbidding stare. In spite of himself, Christopher cowered back. "Go to your room at once and stay there until you have decided to be reasonable."

"Yes, sir," Christopher muttered.

With a snort of impatience, the viscount stalked back into the house.

"Well, that does it," Cassandra said. Her eyes filled with tears of disappointment. "I'll never see London now. There were to be illuminations in the park and balloon launches and—"

"What are you talking about?" Christopher asked.

"To celebrate the peace, ninny!" she snapped. "It would have been *wonderful*, but instead of going to London, I have to stay here and marry *you*."

Well, he could hardly blame the girl for not wanting to marry him. He tried to look at himself through her eyes and shuddered.

"Don't worry," he told her. "You won't have to marry me."

"He'll *make* me marry you, don't you see?" she said. Her long eyelashes were wet and spiky with moisture, and he didn't even have a handkerchief to lend her. "He is my guardian. I will have no choice."

"I'm sorry," he said, and he was.

"I know," she said with a sigh. "It's not your fault."

She managed to smile at him.

"I am glad you're not dead, Christopher," she said quietly. "Truly."

He patted her hand.

"Good-bye," he said as he prepared to leave the terrace.

She smiled at him again, but she couldn't stop the tears from running down her pretty cheeks.

Chastened, Christopher went up to his room like the whipped cur he was.

Two

Cassandra wanted to lie on her bed and cry herself to sleep, but she was made of sterner stuff than that.

Instead, she made her daily visit to the cook to approve the menu for that evening's dinner, and she caught herself suggesting dishes that she recalled were Christopher's favorites, as if in some way that would compensate him for her unkindness.

"Are you sure, miss?" the cook asked dubiously when Cassandra suggested that instead of a dish of buttered peas, of which Lord Adderly was particularly fond, that the cook prepare a dish of cabbage with bacon, which Lord Adderly also liked, but gave him the wind.

Cassandra might be a helpless pawn of the old tyrant in many ways, but she had her own methods of retribution.

As a further demonstration of her pique, she would not do her needlework in the parlor today, as usual, so her guardian could debate with her whichever political issue of the day had got him all stirred up when he read the newspaper. Instead, she would read a novel quietly in her room and instruct her maid to tell any thick-headed male in the household who inquired after her that she had the vapors.

Cassandra *never* had the vapors, and the old man knew it.

As for Christopher—well, despite his words of defiance, she had no great confidence that he would hold fast to his refusal to marry her.

Imagine Cassandra, married to such a pitiful specimen of manhood.

Oh, there was nothing wrong with his looks these days. He was no longer fat. He was no longer spotty. But under that somewhat improved exterior, he was still Christopher, the meek, conciliating mush of a creature she had always despised.

The man she wanted to marry would be handsome, dashing, and masterful. He would worship the ground she walked on. He would squire her to balls and concerts, and take her to London every spring for the Season. She would have a wardrobe created by the very best dressmakers and haberdashers in London. And every other woman of her acquaintance would look at her with envy instead of pity, poor old Cassandra wearing a gown three years out of date the day it left the hands of the country seamstress who stitched it.

But, no.

Christopher was back, and she was stuck with him. His grandfather would insist that the two of them continue to live in this house, securely under his thumb, until the day he died, if the stubborn old man didn't outlive them both. After all, he had outlived his wife, his children, and all of his siblings except one sister who lived in some style in London.

Seething with the injustice of it all, Cassandra still hesitated as she passed Christopher's closed door. She put her ear to the wood and heard rustling noises from within. Was he sleeping? If so, his sleep was disturbed by restless dreams. Or was he just fidgeting on the bed, feeling miserable because of the fate that awaited him?

Perhaps he was still hungry.

She knocked on the door, but received no answer. Perhaps he was ill. She had heard that released prisoners sometimes suffered from recurrences of diseases. She flinched as she remembered how he had examined the sweet biscuits for weevils. Imagine anyone having to do that! It had been all too apparent from his behavior that morning that his experiences had affected his understanding.

She would assign one of the footmen to keep an eye on him for the present, she decided, and ask his grandfather to hire a valet for him. He was the heir, after all, and must be given every outward concession to his position. Even Lord Adderly would have to agree to that.

With a sigh, she opened the door. In the meantime, there was no one else available to look after the poor, confused man, so she supposed it would be left to her. Indeed, it probably would be her task for the rest of her life, one way or the other.

To her surprise, though, no unshaven, dark-haired man tossed and turned restlessly in the bed.

Instead, one of the housemaids gave a faint scream and held her hand to her heart.

"Your pardon, miss," the girl said, eyes wide. "I didn't mean to squeak so."

"That's all right, Betty. Where is Mr. Christopher?"

"Gone, miss. To London, he says. I saw him leaving."

"To . . . London?"

"Yes, miss. He left a letter for his lordship on the mantelpiece." The maid pointed to the folded white paper propped against the white marble. Her face creased in concern. "He told me not to tell anyone he was gone, miss. He hoped to be in London before his lordship missed him."

Cassandra sat down hard on the bed, trying to comprehend the enormity of what Christopher had done. The maid stared when the first giggle erupted. As a rule, Cassandra never giggled, any more than she had the vapors. But she couldn't help it. She recalled Christopher's earnest face framed by shaggy brown hair saying he would go to London to have a look around at all the eligible misses before he made his choice, and she couldn't help going off into whoops. Apparently he had done just that.

"Miss?" the maid said hesitantly. "I couldn't disobey him, miss," the pretty maid said. Her face colored delicately, and Cassandra realized that his lordship's heir had made a conquest. "You don't think I'll lose my position, do you?"

"No, of course not," Cassandra said when she could speak. She picked up the letter from the mantel. "I'll just take this, shall I? And not a word to his lordship or anyone. We want to give Mr. Christopher plenty of time to get to London before his absence is discovered."

Relieved, the girl finished making up the bed while Cassandra took the letter into her own room.

She jumped when an enraged bellow erupted from the hallway.

Oh, dear.

She ran for Christopher's room, and, sure enough, there was Lord Adderly berating the poor maid.

"Why did you not come to me at once, girl?" he shouted.

"My lord, if you want to shout at someone, shout at me," Cassandra said, interjecting herself between her guardian and the tearful maid.

"That I'll do, missy, if you had anything to do with this," he said. He looked around Cassandra to point an imperious finger at the maid. "You! Get out! And keep your tongue between your teeth below stairs, mind!"

The girl fled, sobbing, from the room.

Cassandra sighed. She supposed her guardian derived satisfaction from reducing the maids to tears, but *he* was not the one who had to find others willing to replace them.

"That girl is to be turned off without a character," he said between clenched teeth.

"I will take care of it," Cassandra said, knowing that she would do nothing of the kind. To her guardian, she knew, one buxom country maid looked very much like another. Betty could continue to work under his eye and he would never know the difference.

"What do you know about this business?" he demanded, pacing the room.

Cassandra produced the letter.

"I was going to give this to you," she said. He snatched it from her hand.

As the old man read the letter Cassandra watched, faintly alarmed, as Lord Adderly's face turned an increasingly virulent shade of purple.

Her guardian was the bane of her existence, but she had no wish to see him laid at her feet with an apoplexy.

"He's gone to London!" the old man shouted. "Here. Read it for yourself. This is what comes of your refusal to marry him, you ungrateful girl!"

Cassandra squinted at the bold, idiosyncratic handwriting. Penmanship had not been one of Christopher's primary skills as a lad, and it seemed his years as a hostage had not improved it.

Dear Grandfather,

   I am for London. I am not going to marry Cassandra. Neither she nor I wish it. But, mindful of my duty to continue the line, I will look about me for a suitable bride. It probably will take a long time, so do not expect me to return to Devonshire for some months. When I find lodgings, I will inform you of my address. Meanwhile, I will have all the bills sent to you for payment.

Christopher

Postscript. I took the big, black stallion. I assume he is yours. I promise to take good care of him, and send him back to you when I have purchased a mount of my own.

Lord Adderly was turning purple again.

"That insolent whelp! How *dare* he?" he cried, and went without delay to the stable, where he found his prized stallion missing. Cassandra, rushing in pursuit, found him standing over two frightened stable boys, bellowing at them, with fists knotted dangerously. They were cowering down against the wall.

"Here, get up," Cassandra said soothingly to them. "His lordship will not hurt you."

Lord Adderly gave her the blackest of glares, which she returned with a bland smile. She knew very well he wasn't given to fits of physical violence for all his bellowing, but these frightened boys did not know that. The whites of their eyes showed all around in fright.

"Lord Adderly will not hurt you," she repeated. "Just tell us what happened."

"Mr. Christopher said he were going to London," one of the boys said. "He saddled the stallion himself, because his lordship told us never to go into his stall or he might hurt us."

"And you let him go?" the viscount shouted. "Without a word to me?"

"Mr. Christopher told us not to tell anyone," the youngest boy said tearfully.

"Very proper," said Cassandra, looking her guardian straight in the eye. "You could hardly disobey Mr. Christopher, could you? You may continue with your work now."

The boys bobbed their heads and gave Lord Adderly a wide berth as they walked around him.

"Come along, my lord," Cassandra said, taking the old man's arm and leading him back into the house. "There is nothing to be done about it. The fox has escaped."

"The devil he has, my girl! I'm not licked yet, by Jove! If my grandson has gone to London, *we* are going to London to make sure none of those scheming fortune-hunting hussies get their hooks into him!"

Cassandra's heart gave a leap of elation.

London! At last!

"And wipe that look off your face, Cassandra," the old man said, pointing an accusing finger at her. "You are not going to London to fall prey to one of those jackanapes on the hunt for an heiress. You are going to be sweet and demure and attentive to my grandson, so he'll come home to Devonshire where he belongs and marry you, by God!"

"Yes, my lord," Cassandra said, looking down to hide the triumph in her eyes.

She could afford to be conciliating for now. *Anything* to get to London.

Once there, though, she had no intention of wasting this splendid opportunity to find the man of her dreams by making up to old Christopher.

"I'll tell my maid to pack my things," she said submissively.

Christopher turned heads as he rode down St. James's Street. In his zeal to escape from his grandfather's house, he hadn't taken into consideration that male fashion had changed considerably in eleven years.

The coats he had worn when he was eighteen were of an entirely different cut from those of the gentlemen in the street, and they would have looked bad enough even if they had not been made for a husky young man whose waist was twice the circumference of Christopher's present one. Still, he wore one of those old coats now. He refused to wear the one he had worn from France ever again, even though it fit him better.

His boots were scuffed and had been damaged by damp. He couldn't find a hat among his old belongings, and the one he wore from France was so encrusted with mold he couldn't stand to put it on his head, so his head was bare.

At least he needn't blush for the excellence of his mount. It was the only thing, unfortunately. The sooner he hied himself to a decent haberdasher, the better.

He was slowly progressing down the street looking for a likely lodging place and gathering insults for his pains from the carriage drivers with his plodding progress, when he saw a very pretty brunette being shouted at by a well-dressed male—Christopher hesitated to call any man a gentleman who would use such language in a lady's presence—who lost his head completely and knotted his fist toward her in a threatening gesture.

The woman, far from being afraid, drew herself up to her full height and shouted back. Passersby stood all around them, enjoying the spectacle.

None of my business, Christopher thought. It was plain the lady had matters well in hand.

But then the lady's adversary made the grievous error of putting his hand on her arm and giving her a shake that caused her hat to list to one side, and before he knew it, Christopher had sprung from his horse and wrapped his fingers around the fellow's throat.

"You damnable cur!" Christopher's victim gasped. "Unhand me at once."

Christopher gave him a wolfish grin.

"That is for the lady to say," he said in a low, threatening tone.

"My champion! How marvelous," a low, melodic, feminine voice said from behind Christopher. The lady sounded every bit as good as she looked. And smelled. "Yes, do unhand him if he has learned his lesson."

"Have you?" Christopher asked the struggling man with a lift of one eyebrow. Despite his victim's struggles, Christopher had no problem keeping him confined. The London dandy's muscles were as flaccid as his brain.

His victim nodded shakily and Christopher released him. The man wobbled and almost went to his knees.

"Go away, now, do," the lady said when he looked at her as if he would renew their argument. A threatening step forward from Christopher sent him scurrying away.

The pretty brunette lifted one eyebrow to the by-standers.

"You had better be on your way, as well, or I'll set him upon you next," she said humorously. Apparently taking her words at face value, the crowd dispersed, muttering.

She smiled at Christopher, and his first favorable impression of the lady's looks were confirmed. Her figure was all ripe perfection and sheathed in a sapphire blue walking gown and short, fitted jacket. Her dark hair was crowned by a charming hat decorated with dramatic red silk flowers upon the brim. Her sensuous lips were red, and there was the tiniest of moles at the corner of her lush mouth.

Her perfume was something dark and wicked that made his head swim.

"Sir, are you all right?" the lady asked. Her lovely face grew blurry, and the next thing Christopher knew, he was seated on the ground with the lady holding his shoulders.

"It is nothing," he protested when two burly men helped him to his feet.

"Thank you. I will take care of him now," the lady said as she handed each of the men a coin. "My carriage is right here," she added as she put her arm around Christopher's waist to support his steps. She probably thought he was going to go off in a half swoon again, Christopher thought in self-loathing, like a delicate flower. "Come along, now."

"Ma'am, I am perfectly all right, I assure you," he said in a vain attempt to assert his manhood. "There is no need to—"

"Get his horse," she said to the footman, who helped her put him into her carriage. Christopher sat on the cushioned seat and let his head drop forward

so he could cradle it in his hands. The lady joined him
and settled herself on the forward seat.

"My man tied your horse to the carriage, so he'll be
right enough until we get to my house."

She leaned forward and put her gloved hand on
Christopher's shoulder.

"Are you better now?" she asked in concern.

"I do not wish to put you to any inconvenience."

"Enough of that! It has been a long time since anyone stood up for me in that way. Totally unnecessary, of
course. I can take care of myself. But much appreciated,
I assure you," she said. She gave a long sigh. "That is the
worst of having lovers. When the affair is over, they do
not move along nicely as one would wish."

"I . . . will remember that," he said as he put his
head in his hands again. Why was he so confounded
dizzy?

"Please do not be offended, sir, but when was the
last time you have eaten?" she asked.

He had to think about it. He had spent the previous
night in a stable because he had no money for an inn,
but the stablemaster gave him a bowl of porridge and
milk for currying some of his master's horses.

But no. That was the night before.

Still, he had gone longer without food. French prisons were not known for the efficiencies of their
service.

"Never mind," she said. "We will soon rectify the situation."

Her house was located on a shady avenue well away
from the main streets in what appeared to be a good
neighborhood. The grounds were nicely kept, and
the windows sparkled with cleanliness.

"Come along," she said, taking his arm and towing
him inside.

"My guest will want a meal. At once," she said to her surprised butler. "Bread and cheese will do. And soup, if the cook has some prepared."

"Ma'am, you do not need—"

"Yes, I do need," she told Christopher as she ushered him straight to the dining room. As soon as he was seated, a maid came out of the kitchen with a large bowl of soup and a spoon.

"Begin. The rest will be here presently," the lady said. "You need not wait for it."

Christopher dipped the spoon into the soup and enjoyed the smell for a moment before he brought it to his lips. It scalded his tongue a bit, but he did not care. It was a heavenly combination of carrots, potatoes, bits of meat, and onions.

"Better now?" his hostess asked when he had eaten all the soup and almost half a loaf of bread with cheese besides.

"Much," he said, smiling at her. "And I do apologize for gobbling it all down like a starving swineherd."

"I have not been acquainted with many swineherds," she replied with an answering smile. "But I assure you my sensibilities are not in the least offended by a man indulging in a perfectly healthy appetite."

"I will trouble you no longer, ma'am, unless there is some service I can perform for you."

"The point is whether there is some service I can perform for you in recompense for your coming so handsomely to my rescue."

"Ma'am?" he asked, startled. All at once his sluggish brain assimilated what he should have noticed long before. The lady seemed to be her own mistress and had quarrels with ex-lovers on the street. More than that, she was dressed rather too elaborately for the usual lady of quality. She appeared to be at least five years his senior.

Now that he was closer to her, he could see the suggestions of tiny lines at the corners of her big brown eyes and suspected the unvarying bloom in her cheeks was attributable to the judicious application of cosmetics.

Even a dolt such as Christopher knew which type of lady painted her face.

"No, I thank you," he hastened to add as he leapt to his feet and backed slightly away from her. "I require nothing more. I assure you. Even if I did, I have no money for you. Please, let me go now."

She burst into delighted laughter at his expression.

"My dear man, whatever profession you choose to employ when you leave here, I beg you not to delude yourself into thinking you might make your fortune as a gamester. Every thought in your head is written plainly across your face. I assure you, I am not a member of the sisterhood you apparently think."

"No, of course not!" he said a little too quickly.

"Since there is no one available at the moment to make the proper introductions, I suppose we must do it ourselves. I am Caroline Benningham, a widow, and I assure you that no jealous lover is going to materialize and beat you into a pulp for encroaching upon his property."

"No, of course not," he said again, shamefaced. "The thought did not enter my head."

Mercifully, she seemed more amused than insulted.

"Liar. Well, the evidence is quite convincing, I will admit," she said. "And your name, sir?"

"Christopher Warrender, at your service." To his consternation, he felt his face burst into flame. "I didn't mean it that way," he added.

She gave that musical laugh again.

"Mr. Warrender, you are a refreshment to my jaded soul."

"Thank you, Miss Benningham," he said, uncertain how to take this.

"Mrs. Benningham. I am a widow," she reminded him. "And while I will not claim that my morals are as pure as the driven snow, you are perfectly safe from my wicked wiles, I assure you. Now, in what way may I assist you? Do you require employment?"

"Uh, no," he said. "I do not appear to be quite the thing, I know, but apart from needing to find lodgings, I am perfectly able to provide whatever I require for myself."

She gave his attire a dubious inspection.

"Dare I hope that one of these things you are perfectly able to provide for yourself is the services of a good tailor?" she asked.

"Yes," he said, giving her a wry smile as he held out the voluminous folds of his brown coat. "And the sooner the better, if I am not to be taken for a scarecrow."

The lady's brow furrowed.

"Warrender. Where have I heard that name? Ah, I have it. You are Lord Adderly's grandson, of course! There aren't that many Warrenders about, so you can be no one else. Welcome back to England, Mr. Warrender."

"How did you know?" he asked.

"The release of the *detenus* were a seven-days' wonder in all the newspapers," she said. "Your name was mentioned."

She took his arm again.

"Do not worry," she said soothingly. "I shall not bite you."

"Where are you taking me?" he asked in alarm when she moved purposefully to the door, calling for her carriage to be brought around again.

"To Bond Street," she replied gaily. "Do not look so worried. I will take care of everything!"

Three

Cassandra and Lord Adderly arrived at the town house of the viscount's only surviving sister, Lady Mayville, at an unforgivably early hour of the morning.

After spending one night in an inn, his lordship lost patience with their plodding pace and instructed his coachman to drive straight through the next day and night to London. He would bring his disobedient whelp of a grandson to heel or die trying!

"Jasper, what has happened?" cried Lady Mayville herself as she hurried into the salon where her impassive butler had placed her uninvited, road-weary guests. Naturally she thought that a catastrophe of epic proportions had occurred to bring her reclusive brother to the capital with no notice whatsoever.

"We are staying with you for at least part of the Season, Belle," the viscount said. "You will have to take my ward about in society. Do not bother arguing about it. I have made my mind up."

Lady Mayville blinked in dismay.

"Jasper, what *are* you talking about?" She turned to Cassandra. "My dear, how long has he been like this? I thought it was decided that since you are to marry my great-nephew, you would not come to London this Season after all."

"Christopher, upon learning the fate in store for him, has fled to London," Cassandra said flippantly.

"And you are come in pursuit," Lady Mayville said with a sigh. "Jasper, has it occurred to you that these young people may not be right for each other, and you do them and yourself no good by pressing the matter?"

"Not right for each other? Are you mad, Belle? Their lands march together perfectly. They are equals in blood and station."

"And do not forget my dowry of forty thousand pounds," Cassandra said dryly.

Her guardian gave her a look filled with indignation.

"That has nothing to do with it, you ungrateful chit!" he snapped. "I have reared you as if you were my own daughter. How *dare* you accuse me of having designs on your fortune?"

Cassandra had the grace to mutter an apology, for it was perfectly true that Lord Adderly had been a scrupulously correct guardian except for that one bugaboo about marrying Christopher.

"Where is the whelp? Has he contacted you?" the viscount demanded of his sister.

"Of course. He called on me only yesterday," her ladyship admitted. "I had no idea he was in London without your approval. It seems only reasonable that he would want to enjoy himself a bit before he settles down to marriage, so I thought there was nothing unusual in his presence here."

"Was he . . . all right?" asked Cassandra.

"All right? He seemed to be in tolerable health and spirits, considering his long ordeal. Is that what you mean? He said he has found lodgings and is comfortably settled in. Quite the handsome young gentleman, is Christopher. I would not have recognized him."

"Where is he staying?" the viscount demanded. "I will go there at once and tell him—"

"That he must agree to marry me, or you are going to keep him locked up in Lady Mayville's house and feed him on bread and water until he consents to do so?" Cassandra suggested. "What a figure you should cut if you tried to do any such thing."

The viscount opened and shut his mouth in frustration. That was *exactly* what he had intended to do, of course.

"I feel quite sure," Cassandra said smugly, "that you would not wish to create the impression that your heir is feeble-minded or otherwise incompetent. Keeping him captive here is the best way I know to reinforce that impression."

"Damn and blast!" shouted the viscount.

"Jasper!" exclaimed Lady Mayville, absolutely scandalized. "You cannot use language like that in my house."

"Your pardon, Belle," the viscount said at once. "I am not myself."

"Of course not," his sister said soothingly. "I will have you shown to your rooms so you can be comfortable. You will feel better for a nice sleep. I always do."

"I will feel better for getting my hands on my precious grandson," the viscount said with a clenched jaw.

As it turned out, he had not long to wait for this satisfaction, although when he did see Christopher, it was from too far away to actually get his hands on him.

After some rest and a reviving pot of tea and small sandwiches provided by their kind hostess, the viscount and Cassandra decided to accompany Lady Mayville for a carriage ride in Hyde Park where, sooner or later, every member of the fashionable world went to display their wardrobes and their horseflesh.

A visit from his London solicitor with a heavy envelope of Christopher's bills, which had been forwarded to him for payment, did nothing to improve the Lord Adderly's temper.

"A half-dozen coats," he raved as Lady Mayville's coachman drove the party through the gates of the park. "Three pairs of boots. Four pairs of dancing slippers. Two dozen sets of inexpressibles, three dozen of cravats. Does he think I am *made* of money?"

"Stop grumbling, Jasper," his sister said with a sigh. "A young gentleman about town *must* dress, you know."

"He only has one pair of feet. Why does he need seven pairs of footgear? In my day—"

"Gentlemen wore their linen until it rotted," Cassandra said, "so I daresay they did not need as many sets."

"That will be enough from you, miss," the old gentleman snapped. "Ladies do *not* discuss gentlemen's underpinnings in public."

"Well, *you* are the one who introduced the subject," she pointed out. "Remember, if I were to marry Christopher—which I am not—my blood would be mingled with that of your great-grandchildren. Surely you do not relish such a fate for the poor little things."

"Baggage," the viscount snarled when his sister gave a peal of laughter.

"Oh, do not be such an old miser, Jasper," Lady Mayville chided him. "It is a beautiful day. Can you not put your worries aside and enjoy it? The sun is shining and the air is filled with the fragrance of roses."

"And horse droppings," her grumpy brother added. "The stench from Rotten Row gets stronger and stronger. No wonder I hate London."

He half rose from his seat in the carriage and craned his neck.

"Why are we stopping?" he asked.

Lady Mayville squinted into the distance.

"Ah, I see Mrs. Benningham has her usual court about her," she said. "She can stop traffic in the park for half an hour at a time. Ah, I see she has a gentleman with her. I wonder who he is. Her love affaires are the talk of the town."

"See here, Belle," her brother remonstrated. "You cannot go about pointing out women like *that* to my ward!"

"Mrs. Benningham? She is perfectly respectable, I assure you. Well, perhaps not in the *highest* circles, but she is not a—well, she is not one of the women to whom you refer. On the contrary, she is a widow of good birth and rich fortune. Invitations to her parties and salons are gladly received by all except for a few prosy old bores, I assure you. And her wardrobe is the envy of every woman in London."

"Oh, how wonderful!" Cassandra said enthusiastically. "That is exactly what I want to be someday."

"A widow?" Lady Mayville wrinkled her brow. "No, my dear. I am a widow, and I can tell you it is most unpleasant to lose one's life's partner."

"No, of course not," Cassandra said. "But I should like to have clothes that stop traffic in the park and give parties and salons that are the talk of the town."

"You can do that when you are safely married," the viscount said, "to Christopher."

"Who *is* that gentleman with her?" Lady Mayville asked as she squinted at Mrs. Benningham's carriage, which was clustered all about by gentleman admirers. "Something about him seems so familiar."

"Can you introduce me to her?" Cassandra asked eagerly.

"Certainly, my dear. I was acquainted with her mother years ago, and—" Suddenly Lady Mayville's mouth snapped shut. "That is, perhaps another time, Cassandra. Goodness, how late it is! I will just have the coachman turn around, shall I?"

"But we have only just arrived," Cassandra objected.

At that moment, Cassandra could see up ahead that Mrs. Benningham's dashing curricle had pulled off to the side with her court of well-wishers so traffic could pass. The coachman drew Lady Mayville's carriage ahead, while the lady continued to protest that they should leave the park at once.

"Turn back," Lady Mayville cried desperately to her coachman. But it was clear there was no room to turn around on the crowded lane, and the coachman had no choice but to go forward.

By this time, Cassandra was practically hanging out the carriage as they passed Mrs. Benningham and her admirers. The dashing widow was wearing a delightful hat of blond straw trimmed in trailing yellow and green ribbons, and Cassandra saw that she, and not the gentleman at her side, was the driver. The fashionable brunette carried a small whip in her leather-gloved hand and addressed some remark to her escort.

"What a charming carriage dress," Cassandra said, looking avidly at Mrs. Benningham's party.

"Fripperies! That is all young girls think about," her guardian muttered in disgust.

At that moment, the gentleman at Mrs. Benningham's side turned to face her, and Cassandra gasped as she got a clear view of his handsome face. His hair was neatly trimmed, he was dressed in the height of fashion, but he was unmistakable.

Christopher's hazel eyes widened, but that was his only sign of discomfiture. He gave Cassandra a dazzling smile and tipped his hat to her. She opened and closed her mouth like a landed fish.

"Lady Mayville! Your servant," he called.

"Good afternoon, Christopher," his great-aunt said weakly.

"Grandfather! I did not know you and Cassandra were coming to town," Christopher said audaciously. By this time, Lady Mayville's carriage was drawing away from the curricle.

"See here, you young jackanapes—" the fulminating viscount began.

"Faster!" cried Lady Mayville to the coachman as Cassandra tugged on her guardian's arm to silence him.

"Christopher," she called back, "you had better call on us tomorrow!"

"Today!" snapped the viscount as he shook off Cassandra's restraining hands. "You will call on us *today*!"

"A pleasure," Christopher called back in a tone that suggested it would be anything but.

"I think you are making a big fuss over nothing, as usual," Lady Mayville said with a sigh as her brother paced the parlor like a caged tiger.

"Spending my money to impress that . . . that Mrs. Benningham."

"Perhaps he wants to marry her," Cassandra suggested eagerly. "You did say she is rich. And she certainly seems to be popular."

"Popular!" the old man snorted. "Good grief, girl. Men do not *marry* women like Mrs. Benningham!"

"Someone did, if she is a widow."

"And a rough customer *he* was, make no mistake," Lady Mayville said. "The kindest thing he ever did for his poor wife was get himself shot in a duel over another woman. It was a great scandal at the time. If you ask me, she is entitled to a little happiness."

"The woman's unsuitable," the viscount said, giving her sister a disapproving stare. "My grandson may amuse himself with such a woman—it is all a part of a young man's sowing his wild oats—but even Christopher cannot be green enough to *marry* her."

"Do you mean he is . . . they are—" Cassandra sputtered.

The viscount rolled his eyes.

"It means *nothing*, I tell you. It's all a part of a young man's education. A young man makes a better husband for having acquired a bit of town bronze in his youth. Settles him down."

"*I* need some town bronze, too, then. Taking lovers might settle *me* down," she said defiantly.

"Cassandra!" exclaimed Lady Mayville. "Really, Jasper, this conversation is most improper for a young girl, and it is all *your* fault for putting such ideas in her head."

"That is right," Cassandra conceded. "A lady must wait to take lovers until *after* she is married. No, I thank you. I want nothing to do with a so-called gentleman who has affaires before he is married to me."

The viscount threw up his hands.

"Then you'll catch cold at finding a husband, my girl."

"Fine!"

At that moment, the butler entered the room with a white visiting card on his salver.

"The gentleman asks if you are receiving, my lady," the butler intoned with a straight face.

The viscount pounced on the card.

"Bring the young jackanapes in at once," he snarled to the butler, who left the room with all the speed his dignity would allow.

"Jasper, I will not have a servant left if you will snap at them so," Lady Mayville remonstrated.

"Look at this!" he said, waving the card. "He has had *visiting cards* engraved. And of the most expensive paper, too, I'll wager."

"Well, what of that? One cannot go calling without visiting cards, Jasper!" Lady Mayville's frown turned to a smile of welcome when Christopher appeared at the doorway. "Christopher, my dear boy! Do come in."

She gave her brother a look that practically shouted, "Behave!"

Christopher bowed politely to his grandfather, great-aunt, and Cassandra. It took all of his self-control not to beat a hasty retreat, but he would not give his imperious grandfather the satisfaction.

He reminded himself that he was a gentleman of substance, not a cringing worm, and took the chair his great-aunt indicated. He stretched his long legs out in front of him instead of curling them under the chair as if he had no right to be in a titled noblewoman's parlor.

All the better for Cassandra to admire his new Hessians.

"Are you alone?" Cassandra asked eagerly.

So much for vanity, he thought philosophically.

Christopher smiled at her. She was dressed in what his newly educated eyes identified as a countrified ensemble of blue-and-white striped muslin, but her hair was shining like new-minted gold and there *was* something akin to admiration in her big, blue eyes when she looked at him.

Whoever said clothes made the man apparently was correct.

"Were you expecting someone else?" he asked, knowing perfectly well she was referring to Caroline. Not for anything on earth would he expose his best friend in London to Lord Adderly's unpredictable temper.

Lord Adderly gave a snort of contempt.

"He would hardly bring the hussy here, to my sister's house," he said.

"You refer, I assume, to Mrs. Benningham," Christopher said. "If so, I must request that you take a more respectful tone. The lady has been all that is kind and welcoming to me."

"Welcoming!" his grandfather scoffed. "Of that I have no doubt. You will *not* refer to that woman in the presence of my ward."

"Nonsense! Your ward is dying to meet her," Cassandra said. "She drives her own carriage. *I* shall do that one day."

"That you will not, missy!" her harassed guardian exclaimed. "That woman is not to set foot in this house!"

"Well, actually, Jasper," Lady Mayville pointed out, "she does come here occasionally. Her father was a crony of Lord Mayville's, and her mother and I were friends for years. Hers is some of the best blood in England."

"I do not want to discuss that woman!" the viscount said pettishly.

"I hesitate to mention this, but *you* are the one who brought the subject up," Christopher said. He turned to Cassandra. "Are you having a pleasant stay in London, Miss Davies?"

"Oh, certainly, Mr. Warrender," she said, matching his arch tone.

"Ah, here is our tea," Lady Mayville said, sounding relieved. Clearly she hoped her guests would use their mouths for eating rather than arguing. "Put it here, if you please," she said to the servant. "Cassandra, my dear, will you pour?"

"I would be delighted, Lady Mayville," Cassandra said. She almost dropped the teapot when Christopher absently took a biscuit. "Christopher!" she cried sharply.

He blinked and looked down at his hands to see that he had been about to break it in two. His grandfather *would* have an apoplexy if he inspected his great-aunt's biscuits for weevils. He gave Cassandra a rueful look of gratitude for preventing him from committing this faux pas, and she giggled. Her expression of amusement transformed her face from its habitual sulkiness into something akin to beauty.

"Christopher!" the viscount snapped. "Your great-aunt is addressing you!"

"I beg your pardon, Aunt Belle," he said. "I was not attending."

"It is all right, my boy," Lady Mayville said. "I merely remarked that we have been invited to attend a ball at my husband's cousin's house Thursday next, and I wondered if you would like to escort us. There should be a number of young people in attendance."

"Thursday next," Christopher said vaguely. "I think . . . yes, I am sorry, Aunt Belle, but I am engaged to escort . . . a friend to a salon that evening."

"Well, *unengage* yourself, sir!" his grandfather exclaimed. "It will be Cassandra's first ball in London, and *you* will attend to make sure she does not spend the entire evening lining the wall with all the other misses for want of a partner."

Christopher's eyebrows rose.

"When you phrase your invitation so charmingly, how can I refuse? I shall put in an appearance unfashionably early at the ball and dance with Cassandra twice. After that, I shall go on to my previous engagement."

"You will present yourself here at eight o'clock, sir, and you will escort the ladies to and from the ball!"

"I am afraid not," Christopher said calmly.

"I beg your pardon, sir!" Lord Adderly was turning purple again, but Christopher appeared not to notice.

"I must not keep you," said Christopher, rising. He smiled at Cassandra. "You have much to do."

"I do?" she asked.

"Of course. Dressmakers. Shoemakers. Fanmakers," he said. "And you had better engage a dancing master."

"What are you talking about?" his grandfather demanded.

"Cassandra, of course," Christopher said. He leveled the quizzing glass Caroline had insisted he purchase straight at an indignant Cassandra's countrified gown. It was the first time he had remembered to use it.

Somehow he managed to keep from laughing in his grandfather's affronted face.

"Surely you do not expect *me* to be seen in public with a female whose clothes were made by a seamstress in *Devonshire!*" he exclaimed with a straight face.

"Miss Lacey's in Conduit Street," he added with a patronizing smile to Cassandra. "Just put yourself in her hands, and you needn't worry about a thing. She's quite good at transforming a sow's ear into a silk purse. Not that I mean to say *you*, my dear Miss Davies, are a sow's ear."

"How kind," she said sarcastically.

"Now see here, you young jackanapes—" the viscount shouted.

"And don't forget to purchase a new hat. The one you were wearing in the park today makes you look a complete quiz," Christopher added to Cassandra. He turned to his grandfather. "No offense, sir. You had better get one, too."

With that, he thanked his great-aunt for the tea and biscuits, bowed to the company, and made good his escape.

"Puppy!" Lord Adderly snarled when he had recovered his voice.

"He is right," Cassandra said. "I *knew* my old clothes would not do for London! Lady Mayville, we must go to this Miss Lacey in Conduit Street without delay!"

"I shall order the carriage at once," Lady Mayville said. Her eyes were sparkling. "There is nothing I like better than shopping for new clothes. Do not bother to accompany us, Jasper. You only will be in the way."

With that, his sister swept Cassandra out of the room to leave Lord Adderly to stew in his own juices.

Four

"I cannot like the neckline, Cassandra," Lady Mayville said as Cassandra paraded around the parlor of the very exclusive Miss Lacey's establishment in Conduit Street. It was the first fitting on a delicious ball gown of sea green gauze. "It looks rather low to me." She turned to one of Miss Lacey's assistants. "Can it be brought up a bit? My brother will have an apoplexy when he sees it."

"No, my lady, I beg of you!" the young woman said in horror. "It would ruin the design of the gown."

"It is perfectly respectable, Lady Mayville," Cassandra protested. "It doesn't show all *that* much!"

"My dear Cassandra, you will catch your death of cold if you wear *that* out in public," said a familiar male voice from behind her.

Cassandra whirled around to see Christopher standing not ten feet away from her, looking dapper in a green coat with smooth-fitting pantaloons and gleaming Hessians. His eyes were alight with laughter.

"Come, Aunt Belle, *I* shall be the judge of whether Cassandra's . . . charms are indecently exposed. If you will forgive my saying so, I have more experience in such matters than you do."

Cassandra's eyebrows rose.

"Quite the connoisseur, are we?"

"Quite."

He started walking around Cassandra in a slow inspection of the gown. He pulled out his quizzing glass and stared right at her *décolletage*. Cassandra gasped and crossed her hands over her bosom. For some reason, a gown that seemed perfectly respectable a moment ago seemed quite otherwise under his frank appraisal.

"Christopher Warrender!" Lady Mayville said disapprovingly. "If you have come into this shop merely to put poor little Cassandra out of countenance, you may turn around and go back out again."

Poor little Cassandra could have died of embarrassment.

"Actually, no. I am here to meet someone," he said.

At that moment, Miss Lacey herself came forward, wreathed in smiles to greet him.

"Mr. Warrender! What a pleasure it is to see you again."

"*There* you are, Christopher!" a stunning brunette said gaily as she followed Miss Lacey into the room. She was wearing a revealing ball gown in carmine red with black lace and jet bead trim. The skirt was daringly cut to expose a bit more of her trim ankles than was strictly proper. Lord Adderly was right. Her face *was* painted, although it was done with such taste and skill it was hardly detectable. "I knew you would not fail me!"

"I hope you are grateful, ma'am," he said, laughing into her eyes. "I had to cut short a most satisfying match at Gentleman Jackson's to place myself at your service."

"What a *brute* you are!" she scoffed. "I hope your opponent will be properly obliged to me for saving him a prodigious thrashing. What do you think of my new gown?"

"I find it perfectly delightful," Christopher said.

Of course he did. Cassandra noted sourly that Mrs. Benningham's gown showed at least twice as much bosom as Cassandra's.

"You have such exquisite taste, darling," Mrs. Benningham said as she batted her long eyelashes at him.

The beautiful brunette managed to tear her eyes away from Christopher long enough to notice his companions.

"Lady Mayville! How delightful to see you!" Her eyes passed to Cassandra, and she waited.

"Mrs. Benningham, may I introduce my grandfather's ward, Miss Davies?" Christopher said smoothly.

"Ah, so *this* is the famous Cassandra," Mrs. Benningham said. "What a pretty little thing you are."

She might as well have been describing an infant or a lapdog.

"Thank you," Cassandra said with narrowed eyes. She indicated Christopher with a nod of her head. "What did he tell you about me?"

"Only that you grew up in Devonshire with Christopher, quite as a little sister." She seemed to notice Cassandra's gown for the first time. "Dear me. Are you going to purchase *that?* Hardly the thing for a girl just out of the schoolroom."

"I have been out of the schoolroom for quite some time, thank you, ma'am," Cassandra said with a sweet, insincere smile on her face.

"Well! That puts me in my place! I only meant the gown is a bit . . . mature for a girl of your years," Mrs. Benningham said with a trill of laughter.

"I told you so," Lady Mayville said triumphantly.

"Now she's pouting. Christopher, she's a perfectly charming child," Mrs. Benningham said with a smug look at an indignant Cassandra. "No wonder you are so fond of her." Cassandra didn't miss the quizzical look Christopher cast at his inamorata. "Wait here, if you please, darling. I will be changed in a moment."

"Oh, dear," said Lady Mayville in dismay. "We must go at once, Cassandra. My brother will have an apoplexy if he finds out you have met her here."

"Is there anything that will *not* give Lord Adderly an apoplexy?" Cassandra asked wistfully.

"If there is, *I* have yet to find it," Christopher said.

"Here I am, darling," Mrs. Benningham called out as she drew on her gloves. She had changed into her street costume much sooner than anyone could have expected. She couldn't *wait* to have Christopher to herself, Cassandra supposed. "I shall reward you with an ice at Gunter's."

She took Christopher's arm.

"Lady Mayville," she said with a nod of her head. "It was pleasant to meet you, Miss Davies," she added sweetly.

Cassandra watched the way the woman managed to touch Christopher in many little ways—removing a mote of lint from his coat, touching his arm to direct his attention to a ready-made gown on display, brushing against him as she adjusted her hat—on their way out the door.

Christopher smiled into his companion's eyes and opened the door for her. Cassandra supposed he had already forgotten her very existence and that of his aunt.

But then he surprised her by looking back.

"Cassandra?"

"Yes?"

His eyes traveled slowly from her face to the neckline of the gown.

"Buy the gown," he told her solemnly. Then he gave her a prodigious wink.

Once back on the street, he detached his arm from Caroline's possessive grasp.

"Doing it *much* too brown, Caroline, my dear," Christopher said, amused. "Cassandra is sure to tell my grandfather that you were about to eat me alive in the dressmaker's shop, and I shall be in for a tremendous scold the next time I see him."

Caroline gave a long, rueful sigh.

"I'm sorry, darling. She is *so* fresh-faced and pretty. I couldn't help wanting to punish her a little. I do not believe I was *ever* that young. I would adore being her."

"How curious. She would adore being *you*. She insists that she will have a curricle someday, and drive it in the park as you do. She thinks you are dashing."

"Does she? Well! So I am," she said. "Maybe she isn't as insipid as she looks."

Cassandra gratified Lady Mayville, after all, by instructing Miss Lacey's assistant to raise the neckline on the sea green gauze ball gown. When it was delivered, she saw that the woman in the shop had been right, and it ruined the line of the bodice.

It didn't matter. She knew she probably wouldn't wear it, anyway, because it somehow was tainted for her by Christopher's and Mrs. Benningham's amusement at her expense.

Imagine *Christopher* dancing attendance on women at dressmakers' establishments like the most dissipated of rakes. Did he pay for Mrs. Benningham's gowns as well? *Was* she his mistress, despite everything he had said?

Then the mental image of his grandfather's fury at receiving a collection of dressmakers' bills on behalf of his heir had the effect of putting a smile on Cassandra's face.

It was nonsense, of course.

And even if it were true, Cassandra was sure she did not care in the least.

The night of her first ball in London arrived, and Cassandra managed to keep from wriggling with nervousness as Lady Mayville twitched the small puffed sleeves of Cassandra's gown a bit higher to conceal an additional fraction of an inch of shoulder.

"You look charming," Lady Mayville said. "Doesn't she look charming, Jasper?"

"Charming," he grumbled. "Come along, the both of you, and let us get this over with."

Lord Adderly was still annoyed by Christopher's refusal to be browbeaten into escorting the ladies to the ball so he could spend the evening with a good book and a glass of his late brother-in-law's excellent brandy in Lady Mayville's library. But Christopher had been adamant, and Lord Adderly had had no choice in the matter. He was not about to permit Cassandra to attend a London ball with only his sentimental sister as chaperon.

Cassandra took her chicken-skin fan in her gloved hands and held her head high as she walked to the carriage, practicing the blasé attitude of a young lady who attended balls in London every night of the week. Inside, she was quivering with anticipation.

As a rule, Lady Mayville explained, town would be quite thin of company this late in the Season, but because of the Peace Celebrations, everyone who was anyone was here. If they were very, very fortunate, the Grand Duchess of Oldenburg would attend the ball along with her brother, Tsar Alexander of Russia, the Savior of Europe. Lady Mayville knew the Russian royals had been invited.

"Bunch of foreigners," Lord Adderly grumbled.

"I am so glad you came to stay with me," Lady Mayville said affectionately to Cassandra. "Otherwise I would have stayed home alone, as has become my habit."

"I have told you for years that you should have married after Mayville's death," her brother said.

"Yes, to a husband of *your* choosing, brother dear," she said with some spirit. "The choice of one's husband is too important to entrust to one's male relatives. I remember how Papa voiced his objections to Lord Mayville, and he was the very best of husbands."

"And cut up warm into the bargain," Lord Adderly conceded. "Who would have thought he would amount to anything? A good bit of luck, that, when his elder brother stuck his spoon in the wall and left the title to him. Rum customer, the elder brother. Father had no way of knowing your precious Harry wouldn't turn out the same."

"I listened to my heart," Lady Mayville said, "and it guided me well."

"Do not be filling Cassandra's head with that mawkish nonsense," Lord Adderly said with a snort of disgust. "For every love match that turned out right, I could point out dozens that did not. You'll be guided by me, miss, in the matter of your marriage. Old heads are wiser."

"Yes, my lord," Cassandra said primly, even though she had no intention of letting her crusty guardian choose her future husband.

Lord Adderly was the one who had tried to marry her off to *Christopher*, for heaven's sake, and he had turned into a brawler, a rake, and a womanizer the moment he escaped from Devonshire.

What a disaster *that* match would have been.

Cassandra squeezed Lady Mayville's gloved hand with excitement when the carriage pulled into the line of conveyances in front of the mansion. Fashionably dressed ladies and gentlemen alighted from the carriages, and Cassandra could see the ladies' jewels reflecting the glimmer of lights shining from the candles in every window and from the front door left open to the sultry night. It was quite ten minutes before their turn came to be handed out of the carriage, but while Lord Adderly fussed at the wait, Cassandra had occupied her time in drinking in all the sights and sounds of Mayfair in summer.

"Lady Mayville!" exclaimed their hostess, Lady Houghton. "How delightful! I hoped you would come. We will have a comfortable cose later." She gave a peal of laughter when she saw Cassie's guardian. "Lord Adderly! Is it really you? Lady Mayville, however did you prevail upon him to come? I made sure he would be immured in all his dusty old books in Devonshire."

"'Evening, Gwendolyn," Lord Adderly mumbled.

"Are you still as fine a dancer as you were in our youth?" their hostess went on. "I shall coax you onto the floor later this evening. Just see if I do not! And do not think to hide in the card room, for I shall snuff you out."

Cassandra realized her mouth was hanging open at the thought of her guardian ever being young—let alone being a fine dancer—and she closed it abruptly.

Their hostess gave Cassandra a friendly smile.

"And who is this pretty young lady?" she asked.

"Lady Houghton, this is my ward, Cassandra Davies," Lord Adderly said.

"So pleased you could come, my dear," Lady Houghton said as Cassandra curtsied to her. "I must introduce you to some of the other young people when I am done receiving."

"Thank you, Lady Houghton," Cassandra said as her party took the hint to move on and progressed to the ballroom.

"Woman always did talk too much," Lord Adderly grumbled when they were out of Lady Houghton's hearing, but he couldn't stifle the faint, reminiscent smile that hovered about his usually stern mouth.

Good heavens! Wouldn't it be a remarkable thing if her guardian actually *enjoyed* himself tonight. Cassandra hoped that Lady Houghton would make good her promise to inveigle Lord Adderly onto the dance floor. It would do him a world of good.

"It is all so beautiful," she said to Lady Mayville when she was seated beside her on the chairs lining the wall to watch the dancing.

"Look, there is Christopher!" Cassandra said.

"Where? I do not see him," Lord Adderly said, squinting toward the doorway.

"Ah, I see him," Lady Mayville said. "Coming down the steps, Adderly. Your eyesight has not deteriorated to *that* extent, I hope!"

Lord Adderly gasped, and Cassandra barely restrained herself from laughing.

Christopher looked almost unbearably handsome in black evening dress with snowy white linen—and on his arm was Mrs. Benningham, wearing the carmine red gown she had flaunted herself in at Miss Lacey's dress shop.

* * *

"You are trying to get me disinherited," Christopher said in a low voice to Caroline as he smiled at his hostess. "My grandfather looks as if he would like to draw my claret."

"I could not be remiss in my obligation to Lady Houghton after she was kind enough to send me an invitation."

"Very proper," he said, knowing perfectly well that her desire to accompany him to the ball stemmed from nothing but pure mischief. She had shown no interest in attending a gathering that was sure to be a crush of prosy old bores until she learned that he was engaged to make an appearance for the sole purpose of saving Cassandra from the stigma of being a wallflower.

However, it did him enormous credit in the eyes of society to arrive at one of the summer's most exclusive balls with the dashing Mrs. Benningham on his arm, and he owed the lady too much to refuse her so modest a request as his escort.

He was perfectly aware that it did *her* credit to appear on the arm of a presentable gentleman several years her junior as well—a satisfactory arrangement for them both.

Despite Caroline's bravado and the fact that she continued to be mobbed by attentive gentlemen wherever she went, Christopher knew that her inexorable progress toward the dreaded age of forty had made her hungry for reassurance that she was still desirable.

Never mind that most of the gentlemen in London would sell their souls for an evening of fun and frolic in the lady's boudoir.

It was no small source of amusement to Christopher that every one of these men believed that he had been admitted to this holy of holies and attributed to him a reputation for conquering feminine hearts that was wholly undeserved.

The dashing widow's presence on his arm perpetrated the convenient fiction that Christopher's prowess was prodigious enough to cause a prize such as Caroline Benningham to exert herself to bring this previously unknown country bumpkin into fashion, and he was grateful for it.

Christopher was only human, after all, and he rather liked the way other men's envy-filled eyes followed his and Caroline's progress into the ballroom. Even more gratifying was the way females hung on his every word and fluttered their eyelashes at him.

In the Fortress of Bitche, he could only dream of such pleasures. He had begun to think he would die forgotten in some cell without seeing a pretty woman ever again.

"Well, I had better do my duty by Miss Davies so we can get on to the salon," he said when, as usual, Caroline was instantly surrounded by male admirers clamoring for attention.

"Not yet," she said, grasping his arm. She gave flirtatious little waves of her fingers to the members of her court, promising them she would dance with them all in turn. "The first dance is always for my escort. It is a rule of mine." She lowered her voice. "Let your grandfather see that you are not to be bullied into submission by him."

She was finding this far too amusing, he reflected.

Then he caught sight of Cassandra's eyes upon him and smiled down into Caroline's upturned face.

Let *her* see him dancing with the most exciting woman in the room!

* * *

Cassandra watched Christopher laugh and guide the ebullient Mrs. Benningham in the steps of the contredanse with disgust and longing. She had been sitting here forever with all the other young ladies who were giggling and complimenting one another on their respective gowns, behaving for all the world as if it was not in the least concern to them that they were not dancing.

Unfortunately, Cassandra couldn't follow their example. She knew no one here except her guardian and his sister. Lord Adderly grumbled under his breath about "that insolent whelp" and "that brass-faced harpy," and Lady Mayville was fully occupied in trying to placate him so he wouldn't storm the dance floor and haul his heir by the scruff of his neck to Cassandra's side to bully him into dancing with her.

Where had Christopher learned to dance so well? He had always moved like a sack of potatoes in his youth, especially in the saddle. As soon as the dance was over and Mrs. Benningham was passed to the eager arms of another gentleman, Christopher turned and smiled at Cassandra.

She felt her pulse quicken in anticipation.

Then Lady Houghton approached him with an exquisite young woman in tow. Christopher bowed with every appearance of pleasure and escorted *her* to take a position for the minuet.

"I haven't forgotten you, Miss Davies," Lady Houghton said from Cassandra's left, startling her to attention. She had been staring at Christopher so intently that she hadn't seen her hostess approach. "May I present Lord Whitby to you as a most desirable partner? He is my nephew, so I have ordered him strictly to be on his best behavior."

"May I have the honor of this dance, Miss Davies?"

her companion said with a dazzling smile. How had Cassandra missed *him*? Lady Houghton's nephew was a handsome, magnificently dressed fair-haired man with a slender, bladelike figure and piercing eyes of cobalt blue. "My aunt will only make me dance with someone else if you refuse, and after seeing you, I do not believe I could bear it."

"Go ahead, my dear," Lady Mayville whispered. Cassandra knew it was great good luck to be asked for her first dance by a titled gentleman of such polished address. All the other girls would be green with envy.

Not that *she* was superficial enough to care about such things.

It gave her infinite satisfaction not to have to sit waiting at the side of the ballroom for Christopher Warrender to have the leisure to dance with her.

"I should be most pleased," Cassandra said, hoping that her lessons with the dancing master had prepared her adequately for the task at hand. Practicing the patterns with a candlestick-thin man twenty years her senior and one or two inches below her height would not be the same thing—she felt quite sure—as remembering where to put her feet while she carried on a conversation with this gorgeous golden nobleman.

He was flatteringly attentive—unlike *some* people she could mention.

"You dance beautifully," Lord Whitby murmured. "When I promised my aunt to do my duty to dance with all the young ladies at her ball, I had no idea that I would find the task so enjoyable."

"How very kind," she said, laughing, "when I have stepped on your toes at least twice."

"Did you? I had not noticed," he said, taking her hand to lead her through the next pattern. "When you laugh like that your eyes sparkle so delightfully that I forget all else."

Cassandra's heart soaked up his flattery in much the way a neglected flower raised its shriveled petals to a gentle rain, and suddenly she was not so nervous after all.

She curtsied to Lord Whitby as he bowed to her at the end of the dance. He held her gloved hand a bit longer than necessary, and she could feel her pulse race under his fingers.

"It was the shortest minuet I have ever experienced," he said, and he seemed to mean it. "May I have another dance later? It will keep my spirits up as I do my duty among all the other young ladies at my aunt's behest."

"I should be delighted," she said as he escorted her back to Lady Mayville.

Cassandra was aware that she should have tried to sound blasé, but that was impossible when he was looking at her with such admiration in his fine blue eyes.

From across the room, Christopher watched with narrowed eyes as that blond fellow bowed over Cassandra's hand.

"It appears as if your little friend has made a conquest," Caroline Benningham said to Christopher with raised eyebrows.

"So I perceive," Christopher said.

Caroline laughed and batted him with the tip of her closed fan.

"Do, I beg of you, take that prodigious frown off your face! I could see that Mr. Hornby was going to ask me to dance, and one look at you made him think better of it," she said. "Now, for your penance, you will have to dance with me again."

"I would be delighted to do so, my dear Caroline—later. Ah, here is Mr. Hornby again. I did not scare him off, after all." He bowed to the gentleman and handed Mrs. Benningham over to him with an alacrity that caused her to frown, but he didn't care.

That blond fellow was lingering by Cassandra's side, making her laugh. And Lady Mayville was laughing, too! The opening chords of the waltz had just begun, and that fellow was reaching for Cassandra's hand. She bowed her head in acquiescence.

Christopher quickened his pace.

"My dance, I believe, Miss Davies," he said, taking her hand and positively yanking her to her feet. She had not seen his approach because she was staring into the eyes of that blond fellow, so she was caught off balance and Christopher had to steady her. "Your servant, sir," he added to the fellow when he looked as if he might make some objection.

"It's about time," he heard his grandfather mutter as he led Cassandra away.

Cassandra looked back at Lord Whitby with an apologetic lift of her shoulders.

"That was incredibly rude, Christopher, even for you," she said as he put his arm around her waist. She felt oddly breathless, but it probably was only because he had such long legs, and he set such a brisk pace that she had to positively trot at his side to keep up with him.

"It was, wasn't it?" he said, matching her tone. "The sooner we get this over with, the sooner I will be on my way. I hope you perform the waltz better than the minuet. You were all over the poor fellow's toes."

"I was *not*," she said. "For your information, he said I dance beautifully, and he would have danced with me again if you hadn't barged in."

"What happened to the other dress?"

Cassandra blinked. "What other dress?"

"The green one," he said. "From the shop."

"I've decided to save it for a special occasion," she said, tossing her head at the peril of dislodging the wreath of tiny flowers tucked into her coiffure. "It was much too good to waste on an evening when I expected the only gentleman Lord Adderly would permit me to dance with would be *you*."

He had to laugh.

"That's dished me. This pink thing is very pretty."

"You cannot know how relieved I am that it meets with your tepid approval," she said.

"Who is he?" he asked.

Really, the way he kept changing the subject so abruptly was extremely disconcerting.

"Who is who?" she asked breathlessly as he whirled her in the movement of the dance. Performing the waltz with Christopher's strong arms around her was making her dizzy.

"Do try to keep up," he said. "That fellow with the yellow hair."

"Lord Whitby, do you mean? He is Lady Houghton's nephew. She is making him dance with all the unescorted young ladies. *He* likes my dress."

"My dear Miss Davies, I did not say I disliked it. It is only a bit of an anticlimax after the green one."

Not anymore, she thought regretfully.

"Steady there," he said as the music came to a stop.

To her embarrassment, he had to catch her elbows to keep her from lurching drunkenly about the floor.

He laughed and took her arm.

"Come along, Cassie," he said, and she suddenly remembered the kind, good-humored podge of a youth he had been when she was small. "I'll fetch you a cup of punch. When your head stops spinning, I'll dance with you again and then I can leave."

He probably couldn't wait.

"I would not dream of keeping you away from your precious Mrs. Benningham a moment longer," she said.

Lord Whitby stood up as they approached. The dear man had been conversing with Lady Mayville, she realized, instead of dancing with others. Obviously, he had been waiting for her to return. His eyes lit with pleasure when she smiled at him.

"The country dance is next, Miss Davies," he said eagerly. "Dare I hope that you will perform it with me?"

"I would be absolutely delighted, Lord Whitby," she said.

She gloried in Christopher's look of consternation.

"There you have it, Mr. Warrender," she added with a smile of polite dismissal. "You are hereby relieved of the onerous duty of asking me for another dance. Do have a pleasant evening at your dusty old salon."

Before he could say a word, she turned her back on him and accepted Lord Whitby's arm.

Five

"It is the most beautiful thing I have ever seen," breathed Cassandra as she beheld the almost finished Gothic castle that had appeared, as if by magic, in Green Park by decree of the Prince Regent in observance of the anniversary of the Battle of the Nile and the centenary of the accession to the English throne of the House of Hanover.

The Peace Celebrations were still going on, but the Prince Regent was already planning his next extravaganza.

Lord Whitby put his arm around Cassandra's shoulders to call her attention to a flag flying from the battlements.

Cassandra was aware of everything at that moment—the heavy fragrance of the summer flowers in the sultry air, the pressure of the pebbles on the walk against the soles of her half boots, and the cherished feeling of standing within the circle of handsome Lord Whitby's arms as he pointed out the architectural details of the Prince Regent's magnificent design.

It was early, and there was hardly another soul in the park. Lord Whitby had told her this was the best time to see the castle, and he was right. The morning mist covered the thick green grass with a sheen of dew that sparkled in the sun.

He took her hand in his and led her around the other side of the castle, away from the road, and drew her into the shadow of the building.

"Lord Whitby?" she said in delicious anticipation when he put his hands on each side of her face. He kissed her as if she were a succulent piece of fruit he could no longer resist sampling. One kiss led to another.

And another.

"I apologize," he whispered, drawing back. Cassandra's head was swimming, and she held one gloved fingertip to her still-tingling lips. "You look so beautiful today that I could not help myself."

"It is wrong for us to be here alone," she said, fighting her lethargy. This was a lesson that had been drilled into her from the time she was a child—a respectable young lady did *not* go off alone with a gentleman and allow him to kiss her.

"Miss Davies, your face is the last thing I see in my mind's eye before I go to sleep. It greets me each morning, as inevitably as the dawn sun rises in the sky," he declared. "Have some compassion for me."

At that moment, a curricle swept around the corner of the building, kicking up dust, and headed straight for them. Cassandra screamed, and Lord Whitby threw his arms around her, presumably to protect her from injury with his own body.

"Very heroic," scoffed the insufferable Christopher Warrender. The capes of his greatcoat flared out with his every movement as he alighted from the carriage. The anger in his eyes belied the sardonic tone of his voice. "I'm afraid I must trouble you to take your hands off my grandfather's ward. At *once*, if you please."

"My intentions are entirely honorable. I have Lord Adderly's permission to take Miss Davies for a drive in

the park," Lord Whitby blustered. "I was merely showing her the castle."

"It appears that is not *all* you were showing her,"
Christopher scoffed.

Cassandra wished the ground would open up and
swallow her. From the way Christopher was looking at
her, she must be wearing Lord Whitby's kisses on her
face as if they were so many brands.

Christopher extended one imperious, leather-
gloved hand to her.

"Come along, Cassandra," he said.

"*I* will escort Miss Davies home," Lord Whitby
snapped.

"Not if you don't want me to tell my grandfather
exactly what entertainment you had planned for her
on this little excursion."

"Christopher, nothing happened!" Cassandra said.

"No thanks to *him*! Come along now," he said as he
took her arm and practically dragged her to the
curricle. She resisted, not only because he had hu-
miliated her in front of Lord Whitby but also because
she recognized the curricle as the one Mrs. Benningham often drove in Hyde Park each afternoon at the
time of the promenade.

The disgusting hypocrite!

She was no match for his strength. Her hat listed to
one side as he boosted her into the carriage.

"See here," Lord Whitby objected. He stepped forward as if he would intervene.

"Go ahead," Christopher said with a wolfish smile.
"Provoke me and I will rearrange your pretty face with
the greatest of pleasure."

Lord Whitby visibly quailed.

"I will call on you later this afternoon, Miss Davies,"
Lord Whitby said almost meekly.

"Wise choice. Learn some manners before then," Christopher shouted at Lord Whitby over his shoulder as he drove away.

His expression when he glared at Cassandra was thunderous. She glared right back at him. Then she looked over the side and wondered if she dared to jump out. Christopher's hand closed around her upper arm as if he could read her mind.

"Are you insane?" he said through gritted teeth.

"I wasn't going to jump," she said. "I'm not that stupid!"

"No, but you *will* go off alone with that fellow! I could not credit my ears when my aunt told me where you had gone. You had better tidy your hair before we reach my aunt's house and hope my grandfather does not notice the way your lips are swollen."

"I will not be treated like a child!" she shouted.

"Then you had better stop acting like one. Did you think he took you there so he could pick primroses for you?"

"He said his intentions are honorable!"

"If he is ready to declare himself after two dances at a ball, then he must be a bigger gudgeon than I took him for."

"He thinks I am beautiful."

Christopher gave a long-suffering sigh.

"Don't you know *anything*? Men will tell gullible girls any sort of nonsense to get what they want," he said.

"Is that what *you* do? Escort Mrs. Benningham all over town and tell her she's beautiful so she will let you—"

Christopher's jaw clenched.

"My relationship with Mrs. Benningham is none of your business. The subject is *not* open for discussion," he said. "Understand?"

"Perfectly. As long as *you* understand that my relationship with Lord Whitby is none of *your* business."

"That is an entirely different matter, and you know it."

At that moment he pulled up in front of Lady Mayville's house and handed her down.

"Go inside," he ordered her, exactly as if she were a naughty little girl who had been caught in mischief. "I will not tell my grandfather this time. If I do, you will be on your way to Devonshire within the hour. But there is something dashed havey-cavey about that Whitby fellow. Be on your guard with him."

He leapt back into the curricle with athletic grace and drove away before she could say another word, which was just as well. With very little encouragement, she could have boxed his ears.

Naturally it did not occur to the beastly man that Lord Whitby might have told Cassandra she was beautiful because he *meant* it!

She ran up to her room, relieved that she encountered neither Lady Mayville nor Lord Adderly on the way, and leaned against the door when she was safe inside because she feared her trembling knees would no longer support her.

Lord Whitby had kissed her.

She had thought her heart would flutter straight out of her breast in those exciting moments before that unspeakably rude Christopher Warrender had intruded upon their privacy.

Is that what it felt like to be in love?

Lord Whitby's indiscretion was not repeated for the next week, to Cassandra's mingled relief and disappointment.

He presented himself at Lady Mayville's house for a correct quarter of an hour each afternoon, and he brought her small, tasteful bouquets of summer flowers which Cassandra received with great pleasure. He danced with her at two balls, helped her to all the choicest morsels at supper, and couldn't seem to take his eyes off her when she was dancing with others.

Exactly a week after that memorable kiss in Green Park, he drew her into the shadows of Lady Mayville's garden one afternoon when her ladyship and Lord Adderly had gone upstairs to dress for dinner and kissed her again.

"I could not wait another moment longer to do that," he said as he rested his forehead against hers.

Cassandra pushed against his shoulders to give herself room. This kiss was different from the one in the park.

Very different.

He had forced her lips open with his, and she felt his tongue sweep along her lower teeth.

It felt . . . wrong.

But the look in his eyes was so worshipful, she was sure that she was merely being missish and unsophisticated.

"I have frightened you with my ardor," he said.

Cassandra could only nod at him, even though frightened was not exactly what she felt.

Slightly nauseous was perhaps a more accurate description. Had it given *him* pleasure? If so, she could not fathom why. Perhaps in time one grew accustomed. She repressed a shudder.

"You are so very sweet and delicate," Lord Whitby said as he traced the contour of her cheek with an almost reverent finger. "So beautiful."

He had said it again. Beautiful.

And sweet and delicate.

She rather liked that.

If only he had not used his tongue on her.

"We cannot stay out here," she said, just in case he thought of doing it again.

"Of course not," he said at once. He took her hand, and looking straight into her eyes, he kissed her wrist.

"So innocent and unspoiled," he whispered.

He tucked her hand in his arm and escorted her back into the parlor.

"I would like to introduce you to my parents," he said.

"I beg your pardon?" she asked, surprised.

"Will you come to dine on Tuesday?" he asked. "At my father's house? I shall also invite Lady Mayville and Lord Adderly, of course."

"Tuesday," she repeated blankly, like a complete ninny.

Lord Whitby wanted her to meet his parents, the earl and countess.

This proved he still respected her even though she had permitted him to kiss her, contrary to what Mr. Christopher Warrender Who Knows Absolutely Everything might think.

"I would be charmed to meet your parents. I shall consult Lady Mayville to determine whether we are free that evening," she said, pleased by the grown-up sound of that.

"Excellent!" He squeezed her hand. "I must go now. Until tomorrow."

Bemused, she stood for a moment with her eyes closed, thinking of what had just passed.

Lord Whitby's bride, when he married, would be a viscountess. She could spend every Season in London with a handsome, attentive husband at her side, whose only wish was to make her happy. They would attend all the best parties. They would spend every summer at the seaside with their brood of perfect, golden-haired children. And she would not have to spend another moment of her youth in boring old Devonshire looking at cows and listening to her guardian prose on and on about the proper behavior for a proper young lady.

"Is that Whitby I saw leaving?" Christopher said casually as he sauntered into the room.

Cassandra gasped and put a hand to her breast.

"Sorry. I did not mean to startle you," he said cheerfully.

His eyes narrowed as he examined her face. She averted her eyes, and he caught her chin between his fingers.

"See here, Cassandra," he said, frowning. "Whitby has not been kissing you in dark corners again, has he?" The pad of his thumb brushed her swollen lower lip.

She could not suppress the heat that crept into her face, and Christopher gave a long sigh of exasperation.

"Bloody hell. I am going to have to plant the fellow a facer after all!"

"You let him alone," she cried. "And I will thank you not to use such language in my presence!"

"So long as he lets *you* alone, I will let *him* alone. Don't you know better than to go off kissing any man who looks twice at you?"

"I do *not* kiss any man who looks twice at me. And, for your information, Lord Whitby's intentions are perfectly honorable. *Not* that it is any of your business, Mr. Warrender."

"Hah! Don't be a child, Cassandra."

"He wants me to meet his parents!" she blurted out.

Christopher froze. The look on his face did her heart good.

"His parents?" he repeated.

"Yes! The earl and countess," she said triumphantly. "I trust even you know what *that* means!"

"Good God. Do not tell me that you fancy yourself in love with that prancing man-milliner! I *know* you, Cassandra. He would bore you to tears before the wedding cake goes stale."

"Christopher Warrender," she said through clenched teeth. "If you ruin this for me, I shall *never* forgive you!"

"See here, you little baggage," he began as he reached for her shoulders.

She was staring defiantly up at him when Lady Mayville came into the room with a look of alarm on her face.

"What is all the shouting about?" Lady Mayville asked as Christopher dropped his arms. Cassandra gave him a look of deep reproach and twisted away from him.

"The silly little chit fancies herself in love with Lord Whitby," Christopher scoffed. "He wants her to meet his parents, if you can believe it."

"The earl and the countess?" Lady Mayville's face lit up like a candle. "How delightful!" She raced across the room to put her arms around Cassandra in a rapturous hug. "Of course, you know what this means. My dear girl, Lord Whitby is *everything* my brother and I might have wished for you."

With an exclamation of utter disgust, Christopher stomped out of the room before he could hear more.

Women!

Lord Whitby might have gotten the impression that he could use Cassandra with impunity merely because it appeared she had only one old man to protect her honor.

If that is what he thought, Christopher would put an end to *that* misapprehension immediately!

Six

The sight of red liquid dripping from Lord Whitby's nose was immensely gratifying.

Too bad it was merely the wine that the quaking viscount had been raising to his simpering, well-bred face when Christopher brought his open palm down hard on the table in front of the fellow, making the cards jump on the polished wood, rather than his blood. Christopher was itching to draw the fellow's cork for taking liberties with Cassandra.

Lord Whitby had been sipping claret as he played solitaire. He had inhaled half of the wine and was sputtering about incoherently in indignation as he indicated his ruined shirt.

"Burn it, Warrender! Now I will have to go home and change my clothes!"

One of the waiters scurried forward to mop up the mess as the manager of the club advanced purposefully in their direction.

"Lord Whitby, is everything all right?" the manager asked anxiously. He watched Christopher with some trepidation from the corner of his eye.

Christopher's reputation as a less-than-model prisoner while a *detenu* in France and a favorite sparring partner of Gentleman Jackson caused many a peace-loving man to give him a wide berth. But it was the manager's duty to maintain order.

The man visibly braced himself.

"Mr. Warrender, I am forced to remind you that the rules of the club forbid—"

"Yes, yes," Christopher said, rolling his eyes. "I am not to engage in fisticuffs in your hallowed establishment. Very well."

"Lord Whitby?" the manager asked, turning to the viscount, who had stopped sputtering and was wiping wine from his nose with his handkerchief.

"Do go away, man," the embarrassed viscount said with a wave of dismissal at the manager. "It was merely an accident."

The man had no choice but to leave them, but he turned and watched with narrowed eyes at a safe distance, obviously prepared to intervene to maintain the serenity of his establishment if necessary.

Lord Whitby regarded Christopher with a sardonic expression on his face.

"Am I to assume that you require a private word with me?" he asked.

"Outside, rather noisily, or quietly here. Your choice," Christopher drawled suggestively. He rather hoped it would be outside. "Or I could arrange a friendly sparring match at Gentleman Jackson's, if you prefer."

Whitby visibly paled and indicated a chair at the table.

"Pity," Christopher said with a sigh as he accepted the grudging invitation. "I'll be brief. What are your intentions with respect to Miss Davies?"

"I'll be equally brief," Whitby replied. "Marriage."

This made Christopher sit back in his chair.

"You want to marry Cassandra? Whatever for?" he was surprised into asking.

"Are you blind, Warrender? She's pretty, she's well-born, she's unspoiled, she's—"

"Exceedingly well-dowered," Christopher supplied.

Whitby shrugged.

"That, too."

"And she has the tongue of an adder and is bossy as bedamned into the bargain."

Lord Whitby's fair eyebrows rose.

"See here, Warrender. I'll thank you not to speak that way of Miss Davies to me. One would think you dislike her," he said.

"One would be correct," Christopher acknowledged. "She has been a thorn in my side since the day her father died and left her in my grandfather's care."

"That sweet girl? You must be touched in your upper story," Lord Whitby said in astonishment. "Either that, or you are playing a deep game, here, Warrender."

"A deep game? I?" He reached forward to grasp Lord Whitby by the collar of his coat. "I don't play deep games," he added in a low, lethal tone. "Eleven years as a hostage in France have taught me life is too short to waste time on subterfuge."

The manager started forward with jaw clenched, so Christopher released his victim and made a self-deprecating gesture of apology. The manager stopped and returned to the other side of the room with every appearance of relief as he resumed his pretense of not observing the two men at the table.

"Well, you'll pardon me, I'm sure, for wondering if you aren't so intent upon scaring me off because you want Miss Davies for yourself."

Christopher threw back his head and laughed.

"*Me*? Want that shrewish little baggage for myself? *You* are the one touched in his upper story if you think that! For your information, I came to London to get *away* from her and my grandfather's demands that I marry her. He and the girl's father arranged it all between them before Mr. Davies stuck his spoon in the wall."

"Shrewish little baggage? Miss Davies?" Lord Whitby said with a complacent smile that Christopher itched to wipe off his face. "It is apparent, Mr. Warrender, that you simply do not know how to handle women."

Christopher smiled right back at him.

"God. You deserve her."

"Yes. I rather believe I do," the besotted gudgeon agreed, for all the world as if Christopher had paid him a compliment. Incredibly, Lord Whitby extended a hand in friendship. "Now that you are convinced my intentions are honorable, I trust you have no objection to my courtship of the girl."

"None at all," Christopher said easily enough as he shook hands with Whitby. He noted that the long, pale, soft-skinned hands nevertheless had a firm grip. "But it is my grandfather's permission, and not mine, that you will need in order to marry Miss Davies."

He showed all his teeth in a smile that made Lord Whitby flinch back a little.

"Until the day your betrothal announcement appears in the papers, see that you treat my grandfather's ward with the utmost respect. Be sure that I will be watching every move you make."

With that, Christopher stood and walked out the door.

Bloody fool, he thought as he tossed a coin to the boy who had been minding his horse for him with one hand and accepted the reins of his horse with the other.

The horse danced skittishly under him as he sat in the saddle and fought for calm. He hadn't felt this murderous since the day his old tutor had died of an apoplexy after being manhandled on that long-ago day in France and left a younger Christopher alone among his country's enemies.

The thought of Lord Whitby's elegantly manicured hands on Cassandra made his blood boil with revulsion.

"What a sad waste," Caroline Benningham said with a sigh as she and Christopher passed Cassandra and Lord Whitby in the park.

Christopher and Mrs. Benningham were on horseback, and Lord Whitby was teaching a laughing Cassandra how to drive his carriage.

"Lord Whitby!" Mrs. Benningham called out gaily. "That is an astonishingly adept pupil you have there!"

Whitby's expression was guarded as he looked up in reply to Mrs. Benningham's greeting, no doubt because he feared Christopher would beat him to a bloody pulp at the slightest provocation.

To Christopher's annoyance, Cassandra was so intent upon guiding Whitby's pretty pair of cream-colored horses that she didn't appear even to notice him.

"Madam," Whitby said in what was an unmistakably tight-lipped dismissal to Mrs. Benningham when she would have addressed another remark to him.

"Well!" she huffed when she and Christopher had drawn away from Whitby's carriage. "I suppose that puts me in *my* place. Who would have thought the fellow was sending me flowers and bombarding me with invitations to intimate suppers only a few weeks ago."

Christopher's brows drew together.

"You mean . . . Whitby?" he asked in surprise.

"No, the Prince Regent," she said in exasperation. "Of course, Whitby. *Men!*"

She was so agitated that she drew back quite sharply on her horse's mouth, which caused the alarmed animal to rear up. Mrs. Benningham gave a faint scream and Christopher reached out at once for the reins to steady the horse.

"My dear, you are distressed," he said in astonishment. "Come, let us walk for a moment."

Still holding the reins of her horse, he got off his own mount and helped her down. Caroline slid into his arms and held on to his shoulders for a moment before she stepped back from him.

Caroline walked by his side in silence, looking straight ahead.

"Have I reason to go back and draw his claret for you?" Christopher asked quietly after a moment.

She gave a short laugh with precious little mirth in it.

"I'd be much obliged to you," she said with a rueful smile, "but no."

"What is it, then? Are you in love with him?"

She faced him with a hard, glittering smile.

"In love? I?" she scoffed. "With *Whitby?* Nonsense. One requires a heart to fall in love, and everyone knows the wicked Mrs. Benningham *has* no heart."

She gave his hand a squeeze.

"Do not look so concerned, my dear friend. I am not about to embarrass you by making a scene."

She already had, but he let that pass.

"You have the most generous heart of anyone I know," he said. "So, let us not have any of that nonsense between us. Did he lead you to believe his intentions were honorable?"

"Whitby?" She gave a peal of brittle laughter. "Hardly! His intent was plain and simple seduction. Of course, no man values that which he wins too easily, so I took my time in letting him wear down my resistance. I was on the point of succumbing to his blandishments when your little Miss Davies appeared on the scene with her big blue eyes and milkmaid's complexion."

"My poor dear," Christopher said softly. "You *are* in love with him."

"I will *not* have you feel sorry for me," she said with gritted teeth. "And I am *not* in love with the man. I hardly knew him, except from reputation. He is reputed to go through women the way other men go through cravats. And it is said that he stays up night after night gambling."

"I *knew* there was something havey-cavey about the fellow! I wonder if my grandfather knows about this," Christopher said.

Caroline gave another bitter snort of laughter.

"That's the worst of it! Whitby's bachelor carousing seems to be at an end now that your precious Miss Davies has entered his life. I am told he spends all his time dancing with her at balls, escorting her and Lady Mayville to museums and musicales, teaching her how to drive his carriage, and generally singing her praises to anyone who will listen."

She gave Christopher a brave smile.

"It is only wounded vanity talking, I assure you," she said. "I am accustomed to tiring of my cavaliers before they tire of me. I daresay he would have bored me to tears within a month. But here is another bachelor giving up his wild ways to succumb to marriage with a cow-eyed virgin. While I get old and ugly."

"You are far from old," Christopher said gallantly. "As for ugly, you know very well how beautiful you are so I shall not dignify *that* nonsense with a comment."

"You are so kind to me," she said with a gusty sigh as she looked up into his face.

"Well, you are kind to me as well," he said with a smile.

"You have been exceedingly patient," she said as she walked her gloved fingers up the breast of his coat and rested her hands on his shoulders.

She licked her full, lush lips.

"Come to me tonight at ten o'clock," she added huskily, "and your patience will be rewarded."

Seven

Lord Adderly blustered, he raged, and he even sank low enough to pretend to have the megrims, but Lady Mayville was adamant—there would be no shirking of his duty on the night Cassandra was to be presented to Lord Whitby's parents. She knew very well that her brother, for all of his crochets, had never been ill a day in his life.

Lady Mayville couldn't have been more excited if she had been readying a bride for her wedding. She had been chattering as if her tongue ran on wheels for days. You would think she had been invited to Carlton House by the Prince Regent himself.

"Lord Whitby is the most delightful young man," she said to her brother as he continued to balk. "Such a handsome face! Such polished manners! He is everything you could possibly want as a husband for dear Cassandra."

"I will thank you not to put such nonsense in the girl's head," he fussed. "He is a tallow-headed fop. I did not bring her all the way to London to marry her off to the first fellow who pays some attention to her."

"His father is an earl!" Lady Mayville said, shocked.

"Well, the earl is in excellent health, so it will be a long time before young Whitby can expect to inherit the title and estates."

"You are merely making excuses," she said, "because you will persist in believing you can browbeat Christopher and Cassandra into making a match of it."

Lady Mayville put a hand over her brother's and refused to let go when he tried to draw back.

"You are fond of the girl," she said, "and you would like to keep her with you after your term of guardianship is over by marrying her off to Christopher. You cannot keep the two of them dancing attendance on you in Devonshire forever."

"Woman, you are daft!" he blustered. He looked completely embarrassed. "Mawkish sentimentality has nothing to do with it. Her father and I agreed on the marriage. And their lands match perfectly."

"Children grow up and they go their own way," she said with a sigh. "You were my staunchest ally when Father objected to my marriage to Mayville, and I will always be grateful to you for that. You were the best of brothers."

"I was a rash young fool," he scoffed. "My father should have boxed my ears for my presumption. What did I know of such things?"

"Yet I was happy in my marriage. Few women can say that. Lord Whitby will make Cassandra an exemplary husband. You know she has no taste for country living."

"*Christopher* will make her an exemplary husband. There is no point in dragging me to this dinner, for I have no intention of agreeing to a match between Cassandra and that lovesick young jackanapes. We will probably learn that the earl has gambled away his fortune and the pack of them are after Cassandra's dowry."

Lady Mayville straightened her brother's cravat.

"See here," he complained, batting her hands away.

"Your valet hasn't the slightest notion of how to tie a cravat properly," she said. "You have been moldering in Devonshire for far too long, Jasper."

"This is what happens when a man lets his women drag him off to town."

Lady Mayville's eyebrows rose.

"Let me remind you, my dear brother, that *you* are the one who presented yourself on my doorstep and informed me that you and your ward would be my guests for the Season. But now that you are here, you are going to do your duty by Cassandra."

"I have *always* done my duty to Cassandra."

At that moment Cassandra herself walked into the room.

She was wearing a demure white gown, and her mother's pearls glowed softly at her throat and at her ears. White satin ribbons were threaded through her hair.

"You look *perfect*, my dear," Lady Mayville said. "Miss Lacey is a genius!"

Lord Adderly walked all around Cassandra.

"So *this* is the famous white dress that cost as much as almost any horse in my stable," he grumbled. "Lord! Give your precious Miss Lacey a horse and a pistol, and set her on the London Road. Her talents are wasted as a shopkeeper."

"Pay him no mind, Cassandra. You look lovely," Lady Mayville told her.

"But there is nothing *to* the thing!" Lord Adderly groused.

The butler announced Christopher, who stopped dead when he saw Cassandra.

"Are you going out?" he asked.

Lady Mayville's eyes widened.

"Christopher, you are not dressed!"

He frowned and looked down at his dark coat, spotless pantaloons and boots.

"Am I not?"

"For dinner with Lord Whitby's parents," she amended.

"Lord Whitby's parents?" His eyebrows rose. "Is that why Cassandra is all tricked out like a bride?" He turned to her and smiled. "You want to be more subtle, sweetheart."

She gave him a moue of exasperation.

"I was just telling Cassandra," Lady Mayville said, fixing a stare at Christopher, "that she looks lovely."

Christopher agreed completely, but he was not about to admit any such thing in front of his grandfather.

"She looks well enough, I suppose," he said in a deliberately bored tone.

"Go back to your lodgings at once and rig yourself out properly," his grandfather demanded. "We are summoned to let the earl and countess examine Cassandra to see if she's good enough for their precious son."

"Ah. So tonight's the night," he said. "I wish you a pleasant evening. I have a pressing engagement tonight that I cannot break."

"And I'll wager I know whom it is with," his grandfather said in disapproval. "But this is more important."

"Perhaps to you," Christopher said, "but whether or not the earl and countess approve of Cassandra is nothing whatsoever to me. I'm off," he said. He winked at Cassandra. "Happy husband hunting, old girl!"

"Insolent puppy," Lord Adderly grumbled. "Well, let us get it over with."

* * *

"You look enchanting," Lord Whitby murmured as he took Cassandra's gloved hand in his. "My parents will adore you as much as I do."

"Thank you," she said, hoping her nervousness didn't show too much. Lord Whitby's parents were well known to be high sticklers. They moved in the very highest circles. In fact, his father regularly played cards with the Prince Regent and his set.

The earl's house was a testament to wealth and privilege. Nothing could be more grand than the silk hangings lining the high walls and the brilliant crystal chandeliers set all alight.

The countess actually wore a small, tasteful tiara for dinner in her own home. She gave Cassandra two fingers and a chilly smile when she was presented to her. She inspected her so closely, Cassandra half expected her to ask to see her teeth.

The earl departed from convention and seated Cassandra on his right hand at dinner with Whitby on her other side when Lady Mayville, as the elder and more distinguished lady guest should have occupied that position. Even so, the earl barely addressed a remark to her while he ate his dinner.

Cassandra quickly lost count of the number of courses and removes served at table. Although Whitby was attentive in pressing the dishes upon her, she could eat very little. The way the countess stared at her throughout the meal was unnerving.

"You are doing very well," Lord Whitby whispered to her. He pressed her hand under cover of the table. "My parents like a girl to be quiet and modest."

Cassandra could have wept with relief when the countess stood as a signal to the ladies that they were to withdraw from the dining room.

She soon learned that the worst was yet to come.

"I am afraid I do not know most of my family history," Cassandra said after the countess cornered her and embarked upon an arduous interrogation of her. "I was orphaned at such an early age."

The countess's eyes narrowed.

"Yes. Your parents were from Devonshire, I collect. And you have lived in Lord Adderly's household ever since."

"Since I was seven. Yes, my lady."

"Very good." Oddly, the woman seemed pleased, although Cassandra could not imagine why. "You play the pianoforte and sketch, I assume."

"Yes," Cassandra said, smiling. "Both very indifferently, I am afraid."

"You have had the benefit of instruction, I hope."

"Certainly. I was the despair of all my governesses, alas."

The countess did not return her smile.

Fortunately, the gentlemen filed into the room at that moment and, at a signal from his mother, Whitby went directly to the pianoforte and opened it. With a smile, he held his hand out to Cassandra.

"I hope you will favor us, Miss Davies," he said.

"Well, I—" She looked to her guardian for guidance, but there was no help from that quarter. She had not practiced her music since they had come to London.

"Did you not bring your music, Miss Davies?" the countess asked with upraised brows.

"I had not realized this was to be an audition, my lady," Cassandra murmured.

"I beg your pardon?" Lady Whitby asked, frowning.

"No, my lady. I did not bring my music," Cassandra told her.

"I see. In that case, something simple will be quite

all right," the countess said with a condescending smile. "Have you a selection memorized? No? Well, then. Edmund will help you find something."

Swallowing her rising sense of indignation, Cassandra somehow managed to get through the concerto Whitby selected with not too many missed notes.

And, at the countess's prompting, Cassandra joined Whitby in a duet. He had a wonderful tenor voice, and the inadequacies of her own thin soprano must have been all too apparent, but he gave her a glowing look of approval when they were finished.

"Mother is very musical," he whispered apologetically. "You have done well. Very well, indeed."

The look of admiration and approval on his handsome face *almost* made up for her inquisition at his mother's hands.

Cassandra told herself that her resentment was foolish.

The earl and countess naturally would want to know all about the young woman their son intended to marry.

After all, she was the potential mother of their grandchildren, and the thought gave her a warm glow.

Children. A doting husband. A home of her own in London, one of the most exciting cities in the world.

All of her dreams were about to come true.

"Don't come near me, Christopher," wailed Mrs. Benningham when he had barged on past the butler, two footmen, and the lady's maid, all of whom attempted to keep him away from their mistress. She averted her face from him. "I have heard that measles can be quite harmful to a man's . . . manliness."

"You are thinking of the mumps, I believe, and I have

had them as well as the measles, prison fever, and every other ailment you can imagine, so you needn't fear for *my* health," he said reassuringly as he took her shaking hands down from her face.

"Don't look at me!" she cried. "I look simply *dreadful*."

He smiled tenderly into her eyes.

"Only a bit rosy," he assured her, which was the kindest description he could come up with for an angrily inflamed countenance greasy with ointment. Her swollen eyes were mere slits. "My poor dear. What can I do to help you?"

At that, a tear coursed down her reddened and blotched cheeks.

"I am sorry, Christopher," she whispered. "You must be *so* disappointed."

"Disappointed?"

For a moment he didn't know what she was talking about.

Oh.

Yes.

He was supposed to be devastated at being denied the reward she had promised him for his patience in not pestering her for her favors. But when he had received her note explaining that she was desperately ill and he was not to come tonight, all thoughts of seduction had gone right out of his head.

Oh, he wanted her, all right.

A woman whose every move screamed of sensuality such as Mrs. Benningham could inspire lust in the driest of octogenarians.

But her health mattered most at the moment.

"Do not worry about *that*. Of course, I am disappointed, but I shall live, I assure you. Has the doctor been to see you?" he asked in concern.

"Of course!" she said with a sigh. "Been and gone. And my maid has returned from the apothecary with all his vile potions."

"Well, then," he said, "there is no reason for you to be alone in your misery."

"Quite right," she said with a wan smile. "Cook has already started preparations for supper. There is no reason for it to go to waste."

"Care for a game of cards?" he asked as he opened a box on the table.

She laughed.

"I will make this up to you, Christopher," she said apologetically. "I swear I will."

"Do not worry about *that*," he said again as he offered her the first cut of the deck.

Eight

It was all over town that Christopher Warrender, that dashing young blade who had appeared out of nowhere to dazzle the ladies with his handsome face and the gentlemen with his prowess in the ring, had been admitted to that holy of holies, the Benningham's boudoir.

Why else would he be seen every afternoon and evening going to her house, often bearing extravagant bouquets of flowers? No one had seen Caroline Benningham in public for a fortnight. Apparently, the rest of her court remarked sourly, Warrender was keeping her well entertained.

Money was exchanged over the betting books at White's, although Christopher remained ignorant of this. He hadn't been to his club for some time—not since he had cornered Lord Whitby there, spoiling for a fight, actually.

In truth, languishing in a house full of idle men, drinking, reading the newspapers, and playing cards was hardly his idea of a spanking good time after being held hostage for eleven years in various all-male prisons. The food was better at his club, he conceded, but that was about all he could say about it.

It was more entertaining by far to spend his evenings supping and playing cards with Mrs. Benningham while she waited for her complexion to rid itself of spots so her face was fit to be seen in public again.

"This is all so embarrassing," she said with a sigh. "Succumbing to the measles. How the gossipmongers would laugh if they knew."

She placed a hand on Christopher's, and her dark eyes misted.

"I should have gone mad without you."

"It is not a disgrace to be ill, Caroline," he said with a smile. "You should let me take you driving in the park tomorrow afternoon. Some fresh air would do you a world of good."

She shuddered delicately.

"I would not dare. There is nothing so off-putting to a man as a woman who is throwing out spots."

"Nonsense. They are almost all gone."

She squeezed his hand and let it go.

"I have been a selfish little watering-pot," she said, conscience-stricken. "You have come to the house every day since this whole ordeal began to keep me company, and all I have done is complain. You should be enjoying the pleasures of the city instead of being cooped up here with me. Go. I give you permission. I will be all right for one evening by myself. I wonder that you are not sick of the very sight of me."

"How could I enjoy carousing with the fellows while you are ill?" he asked, and he meant it. "If you stay in tonight, so will I."

"Well, your kindness is about to be rewarded," she said, throwing off the light cashmere lap robe with a look of resolution on her face. "I am still too hideous to be seen by daylight. But there is no reason why I cannot go out tonight to see the illuminations, if you would be kind enough to escort me. I will stay in the carriage the whole time."

She batted her eyes at him, and he realized how much he had missed her flirtatious ways. She didn't seem quite like Caroline without them. She truly believed that the measles had disfigured her, and she was no longer desirable.

If he could just get her out of her house of sickness for a little while, she was sure to recover more rapidly.

"Excellent," he said, relieved. He truly had been concerned for her mental state. "You won't be sorry."

"Now go make arrangements with my coachman while I change my clothes," she said, eyes sparkling with anticipation now that she had made her decision.

One might be pardoned for assuming that the Prince Regent was entertaining a vast army of guests on that sultry summer night, but the slow procession of carriages outside his house was filled with gapers rather than royal guests.

Indeed, His Royal Highness had meant his house to be seen and admired, even though he was elsewhere, attending yet another banquet in honor of the Tsar of Russia.

The marble facade of Carlton House was illuminated with green and yellow flares placed between palm trees in painted tubs in observance of the Peace Celebrations, a wondrous sight.

All of London had boasted such nocturnal wonders in the weeks since the tsar had arrived in London in early June to confer with the foreign secretary of England, Robert Stewart, Viscount Castlereagh, about the political challenges that would confront them at the Congress of Vienna.

The entire population of London seemed to have gone mad with joy!

"Stuff and nonsense," grumbled Lord Adderly, but not too loudly, for Lady Mayville had threatened to turn him out of her house if he did not escort her to see the illuminations. His lordship was especially vexed that his scapegrace of a grandson had not responded to the message he sent to his lodgings that he was to meet them at Lady Mayville's house so he could do the honors instead.

In addition to the illuminations at Carlton House, those in search of marvels sought them at Lord Castlereagh's home, which boasted an immense transparency representing a large dove with an olive branch, and beneath the windows of the tsar's suite at the Pulteney Hotel and that of Frederick William III, King of Prussia, where crowds cheered wildly whenever either of these monarchs appeared.

Although they were still under construction, the marvels being erected at the various parks also had their share of admirers.

What could be more romantic than to drive past the huge Gothic castle at Green Park? Or the Chinese pagoda at St. James's Park? Trees were hung with colored lamps in Hyde Park; lanterns lined the Birdcage Walk and the Mall in anticipation of the anniversary of the Battle of the Nile and the Centenary of the accession of the English throne of the House of Hanover. The celebration would culminate in a splendid fireworks display on August 1, a balloon ascension at Green Park, and a regatta on the Serpentine.

Lord Adderly wished he had stayed in Devonshire and sent a pair of stout bully-boys to London, instead, to drag his unsatisfactory heir back to the country. He had been kicking his heels in London, it seemed, to no purpose.

He found the way that insufferable puppy, Lord

Whitby, made cow eyes at Cassandra in the carriage behind him absolutely nauseating.

"I cannot like it," Lord Adderly grumbled to his sister. "In my day a respectable girl did not go out at night alone with a gentleman."

"It is an open carriage, Jasper," Lady Mayville said for the tenth time. "It is perfectly respectable for a lady to go out in an open carriage with a gentleman, especially with her guardian present."

Damnation! Christopher should be here to help him keep watch over the girl. Lord Adderly craned his neck to keep an eye on the carriage behind him. There! The fellow put his arm around her shoulders and was bending close to whisper something in her ear as he pointed out the yellow bridge ornamented with black lines and a blue roof in St. James's Park.

Some of the couples had gotten out of their carriages to stroll along the bridge, and Lord Whitby and Cassandra, he saw, were about to do the same.

Ignoring the fussing of his sister, who sought to restrain him, Lord Adderly shouted, "None of that, Whitby! You'll keep my ward within my sight, thank you very much!"

"How *could* you?" Lady Mayville said, rolling her eyes heavenward as the sound of laughter emanated from the surrounding carriages. "Poor little Cassandra must be half dead of embarrassment."

"Served the purpose," Lord Adderly growled with satisfaction. Whitby had taken up the reins again and moved the carriage forward.

"Look! It is Christopher!" said Lady Mayville, pointing out the opposite side of the carriage as Christopher drove by in Mrs. Benningham's dashing curricle. The widow was tucked up beside him with a saucy hat and little veil half covering her face. Christopher favored them with an inclination of his head, but quickly put as much distance between himself and Lady Mayville's carriage as he could without risking an accident.

"So, that's where he has been! Squiring that brass-faced little hussy about!" Lord Adderly fumed.

"I will not have you talk that way about the daughter of one of my oldest friends," Lady Mayville objected.

Lord Adderly gave a snort of disdain and returned his attention to the carriage behind them just in time to see Cassandra laugh up into Whitby's eyes with every appearance of pleasure.

The sight did not do anything to improve his disposition.

When next he got his grandson alone, he would burn his ears for him!

Meanwhile, Christopher solicitously tugged the fur coverlet over Mrs. Benningham's lap, and her bell-like laughter floated out on the summer night.

"I am not at death's door, Christopher," she said. "I declare I am going to expire of the heat if you do not stop shoving that thing over me. A fur lap robe. In the middle of summer."

At that moment, the crush of carriages forced Christopher to stop.

"Let us pull off the road for a moment," Mrs. Benningham suggested. "The bridge is so pretty."

Christopher obliged.

"Would you like to get out and walk?"

"Dear me, no!" she exclaimed. "What if someone sees my face?"

"He will bless himself for his good fortune," Christopher declared.

"What a charming thing to say!" She preened a little. "It is the most outrageous fib, of course, but charming, just the same."

He was just about to protest good-naturedly when a pedestrian gave a shout of recognition and reached up into the curricle as if he would drag Mrs. Benningham out of it.

She screamed and batted his hands away. The man's companions cheered.

"Come down, Caroline, m'love," the fellow said gaily, impervious to her distress. "It's been too long since we've seen your pretty face! Warrender can't keep you all to himself."

The fellow was decidedly worse for drink, and Christopher perceived that his two companions were in the same disgraceful condition.

One of them succeeded in half pulling Mrs. Benningham out of the carriage.

"Christopher!" she cried out in alarm. "Don't let them see me!"

She put one gloved hand up to her cheek and tried to hide her face from her assailant.

That's when Christopher lost his head and gave the fellow a cut on the back of his hand with his whip.

"You'll meet me for that, Warrender!" the outraged man screeched as he held his other hand to the shallow wound.

"Go home and sleep it off," Christopher said disdainfully. "I don't meet drunken louts on the field of honor."

He held the whip up threateningly when the other two looked as if they might intervene.

They shuffled off in the night grumbling about dogs in the manger and curst bad-tempered brutes as Mrs. Benningham continued to hide her face. Deep sobs shook her body, and Christopher had no choice but to put his arm around her.

A small crowd had gathered, and Christopher was

trying to figure out how to get Mrs. Benningham out of this mess when a familiar face appeared on his side.

"Is she all right?" Whitby asked. He seemed genuinely concerned.

"Yes," Warrender said curtly. It broke his heart the way his formerly brash and independent Caroline clung to his arm. He had been wrong to coax her into coming here.

"I'll clear a path so you can get back onto the road," Whitby promised, and walked out into the slowly moving traffic so that the next carriage in the procession had to stop or run over him.

This heroic gesture caused mingled curses and gasps of admiration.

"Edmund! Be careful!" cried a familiar feminine voice.

Christopher gave a sigh of annoyance as he looked into Cassandra's solemn eyes.

It needed only that.

She was waiting in Whitby's carriage stopped behind them. She had no doubt witnessed the whole disgraceful episode. Just beyond her, he could see Lady Mayville's carriage and his grandfather glowering at him.

"You will call on me tomorrow, sir!" shouted Lord Adderly.

"Yes, Grandfather," he called back.

Christopher patted Mrs. Benningham on the shoulder and moved the carriage onto the road.

"Much obliged," he said grudgingly to Whitby, who stood there in the glow of the carriage lights looking like a golden hero as he gave him a smart salute. Whitby tipped his hat to Mrs. Benningham, but she didn't look in his direction.

"Do you think they saw my face?" she whispered.

"Caroline, my dear," he said impatiently. "There is nothing whatsoever wrong with your face!"

Then he felt like a cad because she started weeping again. The poor woman's nerves were all to pieces. If she wasn't in such desperate need of comfort, he would cheerfully go find that stupid bounder who had accosted her and blacken both his eyes for him.

They had progressed only a few feet when Caroline gave an ear-splitting scream and threw herself practically onto Christopher's lap. He drew back too sharply on the reins in his surprise and caused one of the horses to rear.

This only made Caroline scream all the louder.

Christopher fought to control the horses. He managed to keep them from bolting or overturning them, but the carriage went back off the road and onto the park grounds at some distance before Christopher was able to bring the vehicle to a completed stop.

"Caroline!" he shouted to his squirming and shrieking companion. "What is the *matter* with you?"

"A mouse!" she cried. "I saw it! It ran across my lap and disappeared into the cushions."

"It's all right," he said as she shrieked again and threw her arms around his neck. She was choking him. "See here, stop that!"

"It ran across my foot!"

The poor woman was practically gibbering.

"Steady on," he said bracingly as he attempted to detach her from her death grip on his person. "I'll find it and let it out."

She shrieked again, and he dove to the floor of the carriage, feeling for the nasty little creature with his gloves.

The things he did for his friends.

Meanwhile, Lord Whitby and Cassandra, Lord

Adderly and Lady Mayville—indeed, most of the persons touring the park on that summer evening—had come to a dumbfounded stop and stared at Mrs. Benningham's carriage as it lurched and bumped.

The springs were squealing so loudly that the noise clearly carried to the spectators. Mrs. Benningham's screams of what they interpreted as rapture made the ladies fan themselves and the gentlemen ogle the carriage with avid jealousy.

"Will you look at that!" snorted the man whose hand had sustained the shallow cut from Christopher's whip. "Damned lucky fellow."

His companion's mouth dropped open.

"Lord, he must be getting a wild ride," he said.

"For the Lord's sake, Whitby," Lord Adderly shouted, "get my ward out of this!"

Some of the more bosky fellows had started cheering and whistling. One of them threw his hat in the air.

Lord Whitby gallantly shielded Cassandra's virgin eyes from the obscene sight as he coaxed his horses back onto the path.

"I am sorry you had to see that, my dear," he murmured.

"I have seen *nothing*," she said crossly.

He patted her hand.

"Your sensibilities have sustained a severe shock. I will take you home now."

"I am perfectly all right," she said.

"Such a brave girl," he said with an admiration Cassandra did not deserve in the least.

She started to say so, but she forced the words back for fear he would think her indelicate.

"A cup of tea at home would be most welcome," she said instead.

Whitby gave a curt nod of assent. He seemed almost angry.

Whitby must be very much in love with her if he became so agitated merely because she had been exposed to the spectacle of a lurching carriage in the dark. In spite of it all, her heart lifted.

If she married him, she need not fear that such a devoted husband would humiliate her with public displays such as the one Christopher and his paramour had put on in the park tonight.

"No gentleman would behave that way with a woman if he truly respected her," Whitby groused.

He gave a snort of derision.

"He'll have to marry her and no mistake after this," he added grimly. "Otherwise, she'll be ruined in the eyes of society."

"He may not mind so much," she said softly. "She is very beautiful. Perhaps he is in love with her."

Whitby laughed as if she had something very, very silly and grasped her hand to place a fleeting kiss across her knuckles.

"You are so very innocent, my dear," he said affectionately. "Is it any wonder that I am mad about you?"

He drove her straight to Lady Mayville's house, relinquished her to the care of her maid, and promised to call tomorrow to see how she did, exactly as if she were about to dissolve into a fit of the vapors after what he persisted in referring to as her "severe shock."

Cassandra sighed.

Clearly, only a woman of no sensibility whatsoever could sustain such an experience without quaking, so she tamely submitted to this condescending treatment.

"Until tomorrow," he said with promise in his eyes as he kissed her hand and sauntered back down the steps to his carriage.

Lord Adderly and Lady Mayville arrived sometime later and, as expected, the culprit's grandfather was in a towering rage.

"I'll cut off the whelp's allowance and send him back to Devonshire," he raged.

"I am as disappointed by Christopher's behavior as you are, Jasper," Lady Mayville said, "but he is a grown man. You can hardly send him home as if he were the merest schoolboy."

"I will, by God! See if I do not. He'll have to marry her else, and I won't have it. Only a completely abandoned woman would make such a spectacle of herself in public!"

"It takes two to engage in such behavior, brother," Lady Mayville pointed out. "He was entirely willing, or it would not have happened."

"You know nothing of the matter," he said. "Men have . . . needs."

Lady Mayville rolled her eyes.

"I enjoyed a perfectly healthy marriage for more than twenty years, Jasper. There is little you can tell me about a man's needs."

"Belle!" he exclaimed, absolutely shocked.

"Oh, do stop being such an old fussbudget!" she said. She forced a wan smile to her lips when Cassandra entered the room. "I suppose we woke you, my poor child."

"I was hardly asleep at this early hour," Cassandra said, scowling. She was getting very tired of people expecting her to collapse just because her guardian's randy grandson decided to make a fool of himself.

"I'll send him abroad," Lord Adderly decided.

"What nonsense, Jasper!" Lady Mayville scoffed. "He has been held hostage in a foreign country for eleven years. He'll never agree to that."

"Perhaps he will. He might find it preferable to being forced to marry that harpy."

"If he loves her—" Cassandra began.

"Love! What does a chit like you know about love? Go to your room, girl, and stop blathering about matters you could not begin to understand."

She would have argued, but she had no wish to listen to more of her guardian's ranting.

Living with him was intolerable.

Lucky Christopher, that he had won his freedom from the old tyrant.

Cassandra had every intention of doing the same.

Nine

It would have been funny, if it hadn't been such a dashed nuisance.

Because of the odd spectacle that he and Caroline had made of themselves in the park, all the world was convinced that Christopher was the most dissipated rake in London.

Unfortunately, Mrs. Benningham was now *persona non grata* in society, and Christopher felt it behooved him to make an honest woman of her. He supposed he should be glad she had no close male relatives jealous enough of her honor to challenge him to a duel.

He presented himself at her house at noon the next day, freshly barbered and dressed to the nines. This was not a love match, but he felt he owed it to Mrs. Benningham to at least *look* the part of an adoring swain. He carried a big bouquet of orchids, which he had procured at exorbitant expense and great trouble.

So, he might be pardoned for being vexed when the woman for whose honor he was prepared to make the ultimate sacrifice laughed herself into stitches at the sight of him.

"I fail to see what you find so amusing, madam," he said coldly after he begged her to make him the happiest of men.

"Oh, Kit!" she cried, running to him and kissing him on each cheek. "Was ever a man so absurd?"

Christopher blinked in consternation.

He had expected to find her dissolved in tears of despair and humiliation, and hiding in her house with all the draperies drawn.

Instead, she was dressed for a day on the town in a smart carriage dress. She looked well rested, and he could only feel resentful. *He* had been awake all night, contemplating the prospect of marriage with her.

"Darling Kit, it is apparent that you have had little experience in living down scandals," she said as she took the flowers. "How lovely! I do adore orchids. Especially when they are the gift of a handsome man."

She handed them to her maid to put in water.

"I have already ordered the carriage. You may accompany me, if you wish. In fact, that would be best, all things considered."

"Where are we going?" he asked, all at sea.

She was the damnedest wronged woman he had ever seen.

"Shopping," she said with uplifted eyebrows. "The sooner I am seen abroad, going about my business, the better."

She made a small, flirtatious moue at him.

"How unfortunate that I still look so dreadful."

He might be taken entirely off balance, but Christopher knew what was expected of him.

"You look beautiful," he said.

She frowned into a mirror and adjusted some of the curls on her brow.

"Well, at least the spots are gone, although they have left my skin a bit puffy."

It was on the tip of his tongue to say the cosmetics

hid the defects of her complexion admirably, but he wasn't *that* much of a clod. He knew very well that a gentleman is not supposed to notice such arts.

"You look beautiful," he said again, but he couldn't stop a chuckle from escaping.

Mrs. Benningham laughed up at him.

"You are an apt pupil," she said, batting him on the arm with her gloved fingers.

Indeed, she had told him early in their association that "You look beautiful" is the safest response a gentleman can make when he finds himself in any volatile situation with a lady.

She gave her coiffure a last satisfied pat.

"Come along, then. Another lesson for you, Christopher. When you have disgraced yourself in public, staying behind closed doors and refusing to receive visitors is tantamount to an admission of guilt. Absolutely *fatal*, my dear."

"Is it?" he asked, fascinated.

"Yes. The best thing is to get out in public immediately and behave as if we have done absolutely nothing wrong—which, indeed, we have not. Let us go to Miss Lacey's first." She took a deep breath of anticipation. Her dark eyes gleamed. "Ah, the shops! How I have missed them!"

"My dear Mrs. Benningham," he said, laughing. "How I have missed *you*!"

Indeed, the lachrymose female who had spent the past two weeks bemoaning her ruined looks had magically disappeared.

"I came at once to give you my sympathy and support," Lord Whitby said, for all the world as if there had been a death in the family, when he called upon

Cassandra the afternoon after the debacle in the park.

Lady Mayville looked gratified, Lord Adderly scowled, and Cassandra was trying very hard not to feel resentful, even though Lord Whitby had presented her with a lavish bouquet of plump pink roses.

It was rather high-handed of him, she thought, to take the roses away again before she barely had a chance to sniff them, and hand them to a maid with instructions to put them in water immediately and set them in the entrance hall with his card prominently displayed.

Plainly Lord Whitby believed that she, Lord Adderly, and Lady Mayville were in disgrace because of their relationship with Christopher, and association with *him* would be enough to return them to respectability.

"The important thing is to protect Miss Davies's reputation, which is not an insurmountable task because she has no blood relationship with Mr. Warrender," he said. "You may depend upon me to do all I can to mitigate the damage, and I have engaged my mother to do so as well. We shall brush through the business tolerably well, never fear."

Cassandra found it difficult to utter the expressions of gratitude he so plainly expected, but she needn't have worried.

Lady Mayville was effusive enough for them both.

"Oh, Lord Whitby!" that lady exclaimed. "What a friend you are to us!"

Lord Adderly, of course, was in his habitual preapoplectic state because of a message he had received earlier that morning from his unsatisfactory grandson, informing his lordship that he intended to offer for Mrs. Benningham and he expected Lord

Adderly to welcome her into the family with every attention due the prospective wife of his heir.

"There, there, my lady," Lord Whitby said bracingly as he took Lady Mayville's hands in both of his. "All will be well, I promise you."

His manner toward the elder lady was so kind that Cassandra felt her resentment lessen.

He was only trying to help, after all.

It was not fair to blame *him* because Christopher had plunged himself into scandal.

"What is required is a show of confidence," Lord Whitby said with a brilliant smile at Cassandra. "We will go riding in the park."

"A splendid idea," said Lady Mayville. "Run along and change into your new riding dress, my dear. The one with the Kutusoff hat."

Because she seemed to have been left with no choice, Cassandra obeyed.

It is an odd world, Christopher reflected as he drove Mrs. Benningham through the park.

The high sticklers, it was true, gave them the cut direct, but all of Mrs. Benningham's usual court seemed to have turned out in force.

Christopher could only marvel at the lady. In a peculiar way, he was proud of her.

With magnificent unconcern, she acknowledged a smattering of applause that broke out when they rode past a grouping of the wildest rakes in town, although she did not deign to speak to any of them.

There were levels, she haughtily informed the bemused Christopher, to which even *she* did not stoop.

"Such a grand fuss over nothing," she told one of her chronic admirers who had the temerity to make a veiled reference to last night's folly. "A mouse got into the carriage, you see, and I made such a fuss that poor Mr. Warrender temporarily lost control of the horses. So silly of me. But the little creature had somehow gotten under my skirt and, well, I would not be the first woman to make a ridiculous spectacle of herself over a mouse!"

Christopher could see from the knowing expressions on the other men's faces that they did not believe a word of it. Indeed, in their place he doubted if *he* would.

When the same gentleman said that he supposed now that Christopher, the fortunate dog, would be leading Mrs. Benningham to the altar, the lady erupted into trills of laughter.

"Marry poor Mr. Warrender!" she cried. "How absurd! Can you see *me* acting the role of a complaisant little wife? Certainly you do not expect me to chain myself to a husband merely because of a silly misunderstanding. You have been about the world long enough to know, my dear Mr. Creevey, that the gossipmongers *will* make something of nothing and all we can do is laugh at their foolishness until the whole thing blows over."

Since Mr. Creevey was a notorious gossip whose talent for ferreting out scandal had made him a popular dinner guest at all the finest houses in London, he was silenced.

Temporarily, at least.

Christopher had no delusions that this was the last word on the matter.

Indeed, the sly looks he found directed at him from other gentlemen made him long to plant someone— at this point, he cared not whom—a facer to relieve his frustration.

He could only be relieved that Mrs. Benningham did not expect him to marry her. After eleven years in captivity, he was hardly ready to give up his freedom. But he didn't appreciate being the butt of every crude jokester in town, either.

Incredibly, though, Mrs. Benningham gave every appearance of enjoying herself. She was either very courageous or every bit as abandoned as his grandfather thought.

His grandfather.

Christopher shuddered to think what *he* would have to say to all this.

He smiled mechanically at Mrs. Benningham's jests and tried to match his companion's carefree manner. He could not wait to return Mrs. Benningham to her home so he could get the dreaded interview with his grandfather over with.

But he was mistaken in thinking the worst was over, for just as Mrs. Benningham had determined they had made their statement to society and could safely leave the park, they encountered Lord Whitby and Cassandra on horseback.

Cassandra looked severe in a military cut riding habit, and the expression on her face was no less welcoming.

"Miss Davies. Lord Whitby," called Mrs. Benningham with a wave of her uplifted hand. She seemed determined to brazen it out to the end. "Beautiful day, is it not?"

Whitby merely stared at the lady and made it obvious that he was aligned firmly with the ranks of those who did not intend to recognize Mrs. Benningham in public this day.

It made Christopher's spirits sink even lower, not because he gave a rap what Whitby thought, but because he knew his grandfather probably was making Cassandra's and Lady Mayville's lives miserable over this situation.

To his astonishment, Cassandra stopped her horse and looked directly at him. She gave him a nod, which he solemnly returned.

Then her eyes shifted to his companion.

"A lovely day, indeed," Cassandra said to Mrs. Benningham. The smile that accompanied this remark did not reach her eyes, but that hardly mattered.

Christopher heard a chorus of intaken breaths from behind him, and no wonder.

Cassandra had acknowledged the disgraced woman in public. She had refused to take the sensible course and pretend she didn't know her. It remained to be seen how it would affect her own precarious position in society.

"Miss Davies," hissed Whitby in disapproval as he reached out to take her reins and lead her away.

Cassandra calmly took the reins back and gave him a straight look, but she moved on.

"Well," said Mrs. Benningham with upraised eyebrows, "I must say there appears to be more to your Miss Davies than meets the eye."

Indeed, Christopher himself was beginning to think so.

"Your compassion does you much honor," Lord Whitby said as he guided Cassandra further into the park, away from the disgraced couple in the curricle.

Cassandra did not make the error of mistaking this statement for a compliment, and she would not pretend she had.

"My foolishness, you mean," she said. "Do you think I do not know what you are thinking?"

"Then why did you do it?" he demanded. His voice was lowered to prevent others from overhearing their conversation, but it was no less accusing. "If this comes to my mother's ears, she will be most displeased."

"She is *your* mother, not mine," she snapped.

"Mother's influence in society is enormous. There was every hope you could emerge from this scandal unscathed if you had followed my sensible advice and restrained from recognizing either Mr. Warrender or Mrs. Benningham in public. Disassociating yourself from them in the eyes of society is of crucial importance, but you have *spoken* to her."

"I fail to see what business it is of yours, Lord Whitby," Cassandra said coldly. He reached out toward her in appeal, but she turned away from him.

"Cassandra, my darling," he said, sounding heartbroken. "I see I have offended you, and that was not my intention."

"How could I not be offended when you take me to task as if I were a naughty girl because I refused to cut my guardian's grandson in public? I have known him all my life."

"It is the lady whom you did not cut in public," he said. "There is a difference."

"I must be very stupid, then, for I fail to see it!"

"Let us walk awhile," he said, taking her reins again and guiding them both to the side of the road.

She almost snatched them back. However, she realized this would be childish, so she allowed him to help her down from her mount.

"Do not frown at me so, Cassandra," he said softly as he gazed into her eyes. "I cannot bear it."

She accepted his arm and took the reins of her horse in her free hand. He did the same, so they strolled between the two horses. The animals, therefore, would provide a sort of living screen between them and the other visitors to the park.

"I have something most particular to ask you," he said, looking at the ground. "This is hardly the most ideal of circumstances, but I see I must make my feelings plain to you so you will understand why I am so jealous of your reputation."

He gazed at her with those mesmerizing blue eyes, and when he spoke there was not a hint of condescension in his voice.

He seemed almost humble.

"I love you, Cassandra," he said simply. "I want to marry you. I would have spoken to your guardian soon. Indeed, I had already broached the matter to my parents, and gained their approval."

"Lord Whitby, I—"

"Please," he said, "allow me to finish. My parents are very proud. Too proud, you would say, and be perfectly correct. Can you understand that I am near mad with worry that my parents will withdraw their approval?"

"I . . . I don't know what to say."

"Of course you don't," he said ruefully. "It is much too soon. We should have danced at a greater number of balls together. There should have been further intercourse between our families, perhaps dinners exchanged a few times among my parents, your guardian and Lady Mayville while you and I determined whether we would suit. But now everything is changed."

"I . . . see," she said. Her mind was whirling. He was in love with her. He wanted to marry her. She had expected this. *Prayed* for this. But still it was a shock.

"Do not give me your answer yet," he continued, although the congratulatory expression on his face indicated he was in no doubt of her eventual acceptance.

"You must think me very foolish that I do not know my own mind, but—"

"Silence, my pet," he said lovingly. "Did I not say you need not give me your answer yet?"

My pet?

Cassandra bit back the sharp rejoinder that had instantly sprung to her tongue. My pet, indeed!

Oblivious to his *gaffe*, he smiled beatifically at her.

"We will speak of it again after I have spoken to Lord Adderly."

"I think I want to leave now," she said. She turned toward her horse, and he took the hint to assist her into the saddle.

"Of course. You have much to think about," he said gravely. He took her hands and gazed up at her, every inch the ardent swain.

"Do not let worry cloud your beautiful eyes, my dear," he added. "All will be well, I promise you. Just dream of the day when we are seated by our hearth with our children all about us, and that will sustain you."

Children.

Oh, my.

Cassandra, apparently, had achieved every maiden's goal upon embarking upon her first Season in London—a handsome suitor with a title and an impeccable position society.

Lady Mayville would be ecstatic. Her acquaintances in Devonshire would be pea green with envy.

Cassandra, if she accepted him, was about to step upon the threshold of an exciting new life, a life in which she would be admired and have every whim indulged by an adoring husband.

She would have a real family, at last, and the void that had been left in her heart with the death of her parents would be filled to the brim with happiness.

It was her every dream come true. Lord Whitby was certainly right about that.

So, why did she feel so confused that she wanted to throw herself upon her bed and weep for hours?

Indeed, she could feel those tears in her eyes already, and she tried in vain to hide them from Lord Whitby.

"There, there, darling," he said fondly.

"I am sorry." She sniffed. "I do not know what has come over me."

"Silly girl," he said with a smug smile on his face. "You need not apologize. Tears of happiness are perfectly appropriate on such an occasion."

Ten

Cassandra looked up at Christopher with tear-swollen eyes when he entered the parlor, hat in hand.

"My poor girl," he said, feeling terrible for causing her such distress. "I should have known my grandfather would make *you* miserable over *my* indiscretion."

Her chin went up.

"You mistake the matter," she said. "What you do is no business of mine. Lord Adderly is waiting for you in the library. I should not keep him waiting any longer, if I were you."

"I shall enter the lion's den in a moment. Cassandra," he said, "I truly appreciate what you did in the park today. It took courage to speak to Mrs. Benningham and me in the teeth of society's disapproval."

She gave him a negligent shrug.

"It is not Mrs. Benningham's fault or yours that people *will* talk."

"For your information—not that I expect you to believe me—it was not what it appeared. That is to say, we weren't . . . we didn't . . ."

"What *was* it then?" she asked.

Amazing. She looked as if she honestly wanted to know.

"It was a mouse. I have no idea how the creature got into the carriage, but it went under her skirt." He gave

a harsh bark of laughter at her look of utter in-
credulity. "I do not expect you to believe me. No one
else does."

She considered him for a moment.

"Actually," she said deliberately, "I do."

"I beg your pardon?"

It was the last thing he expected her to say.

"You forget, I have known you since you were a
clumsy boy, and this is *precisely* the sort of thing that
happens to you. You may be less clumsy now. But
considering that you managed to end up in a series
of French prisons merely because you happened to
go abroad with your tutor at the wrong time, and
considering that you manage to end up in your grandfather's black books *whatever* you do, I would say your
luck has not changed with adulthood."

She actually smiled at him, a real smile full of
amusement. It took his breath away.

She *believed* him.

"It is indelicate of me to point this out, I know," she
continued. "But only you would manage to find yourself in a carriage at night with a mouse and a female
screaming her head off with scores of witnesses looking on as the carriage bounces and squeaks. Lord
Adderly may think you are a heartless rake and dead
to all decency, but *I* think not even *you* would be so
overcome with lust that you would choose to exercise
it on the poor woman in such surroundings."

"Cassandra, you are the *only* one who believes me,"
he said. "I could kiss you!"

She drew back with a look of comical dismay on her
face.

"I pray you will not! Heaven only knows what terrible thing will happen to me, if you do! Poor Mrs.
Benningham."

"You are a great gun, Cassandra," he said, grinning. "Whoever would have thought it?"

She grinned back at him, then their smiles faded. For a moment there, he *did* want to kiss her, and she seemed to have realized it at the same time.

Cassandra averted her eyes.

"You had better go see your grandfather," she said.

He took a deep breath and braced himself.

"I am afraid so," he said with a sigh.

He hesitated.

"You were crying just now when I walked in."

"It is nothing, Christopher. I merely had something in my eye." She smiled a little too brightly at him. "Stop stalling, now. Go see Lord Adderly. In a moment *you* will be the one in tears."

She had to remind him.

Lord, had he actually wanted to kiss *Cassandra?*

The coming ordeal obviously had unhinged his mind.

Before Christopher could say a word, his grandfather walked right up to him and poked him in the chest with a gnarled forefinger.

"You are *not* going to marry that shameless hussy," he barked.

"But, I—"

"That is all I have to say on the matter!"

"But, I—"

"My word is final. I do not approve of your carousing, but I can overlook it. I sowed plenty of wild oats when I was your age, and there is no reason why you cannot do the same before you settle down to marriage."

"But, I—"

"You may think you are in love with her—"

"I hold Mrs. Benningham in the greatest esteem, but I am not in love with her."

Lord Adderly regarded him with something that might have been approval.

"Well, at last you are showing some sense," he said. "But why did you have to give that graphic demonstration of animal prowess in the park? Can't you save that sort of thing for when you are decently indoors?"

"I did not demonstrate animal prowess or anything else," he said. "A mouse ran under her skirt, and I was merely trying to capture it so I could get it out of the carriage."

The old man gave a bark of humorless laughter.

"Do not insult my intelligence with that faradiddle, boy," he said. "I'd think better of you for owning up to your indiscretion."

"If it were true, I would be honor-bound to offer for Mrs. Benningham, do you not agree?"

"You are not going to marry that woman!" Lord Adderly shouted. "I won't have it, I tell you!"

"No reason to shatter the windows," Christopher said glumly. "I asked her and she laughed in my face. I felt like a fool."

"I wonder what game she is playing," the old man said. "I don't trust her."

"No game. She values her freedom as much as I value mine."

"The woman is mad, but that is to the good," Lord Adderly said thoughtfully. "Very well, then. No harm done. I trust you have cut the connection. In public, I mean."

"Cut the connection? Whatever do you mean?"

"Well, after this you can hardly be seen in public with the woman. But what you do with her behind closed doors is no one's business. I do not mean to be unreasonable."

"*That* would be a novelty," Christopher muttered.

"All that is required is a bit of discretion. You may continue to diddle the widow with my goodwill as long as you no longer associate with her in public."

"Mrs. Benningham is my friend, and she has done nothing wrong," Christopher said.

"The woman has exposed herself to the censure of society."

"The woman has exposed herself to nothing," Christopher said wryly, "including me."

"There's no reason to be crass—what did you say?" Lord Adderly asked, taken aback. "Are you saying you have not . . . that she did not . . ."

"That is exactly what I have been saying."

"But everyone knows you have spent every evening with her in her house for two weeks. What *else* have you been doing all that time?"

"Not what you think, more's the pity," Christopher said dryly.

"Whoever would have thought you would turn out to be such an accomplished liar," Lord Adderly scoffed.

"Whoever would have thought," Christopher replied, "that a man so steeped in morality would have such a filthy mind. Honestly, the woman was ill. She had the measles. She did not want to be seen abroad looking less than her best, and she begged me to keep her secret because she thought the news would expose her to ridicule."

"And you were just there to hold her hand and drink tea with her," the viscount said sarcastically.

"No."

"Aha!"

"We played cards, too."

Lord Adderly took a deep breath for calm. It apparently didn't help. It was plain the old man didn't believe a word of it.

"Get out of my sight," he said through gritted teeth. At last.

Christopher was quick to comply.

When he escaped from the library, he found Cassandra waiting for him.

"Are you all right?" she asked. "I heard him shouting all the way to the parlor."

Christopher smiled.

"Yes, thank you for asking. He ranted. He raved. But he could hardly do more than that."

"Have you succeeded in sending him off in an apoplexy this time?"

"His luck holds firm," Christopher acknowledged.

"I am relieved to hear it."

She hesitated on the point of saying something else.

"What is it, Cassandra?" he asked. She looked troubled, and he doubted it had anything to do with the fact that his grandfather was angry with him.

"Nothing," she said, forcing a smile. "Nothing at all."

He was doubtful, but she turned away from him and went down the hall.

Peculiar.

It was unlike Cassandra not to speak her mind.

"Cassandra!" he called out as he followed her. When she didn't stop, he caught her arm and she turned to look at him.

She *was* crying.

"Tell me what is wrong," he said. He drew her into one of the parlors.

She wiped away her tears with the back of one hand and sat down on the sofa. He sat next to her and took both of her hands in his.

"You can tell me," he coaxed. "I have known you since you were a scrubby brat, and you have known me since I was a fat, spotty youth. You've said so yourself."

This made her smile.

"You will only laugh at me," she said as she looked at him with all the earnestness in her soul, "but I truly believe that it is important for one to be in love with the man one marries. One shouldn't promise to honor a man and bear his children unless one's heart is engaged. Do you understand what I mean?"

"Oh, I see." He rolled his eyes. "Grandfather has been at you again about marrying me. Am I correct?"

"Well, yes. He is *always* at me about marrying you, but—"

"Cassandra, Cassandra," he said, shaking his head. "Let us make a pact right now."

Christopher framed her face in his hands, and her lips parted as she stammered into silence. Her skin was so soft, and her eyes were rimmed in red. The tip of her nose was pink.

He could not bear to see her in such distress.

"My grandfather cannot force you to marry someone you do not want. Remember that. The Medieval days when a guardian could drug a maiden and force her to the altar and say her vows for her are gone." He took both of her hands in his again. "As long as you remain steadfast and refuse to marry me, he cannot force you to it."

"But, I—"

"And I will do the same by you," he continued. "No matter how he tries to browbeat me, I will *not* agree to marry you. You will be sought out by many men for your fortune, Cassandra. And the fact that you are an attractive girl will only be an added incentive to them."

"Do you really think so? That I am attractive?"

"*Very* attractive," he said. "I would not have recognized you at all if it hadn't been for your squabbish little snub of a nose."

Actually, he adored her upturned nose. But he could hardly tell her that. How she would stare at him.

And it certainly would make her even more fearful that she might end up shackled to him for life, poor girl. He hastened to reassure her.

"About our pact. Do you accept?"

"Of course," she said after searching his face for a moment.

"There you are then," he said as he squeezed her hand. "You needn't fear the terrible fate of marrying me."

He gave a long sigh.

"What a day," he said ruefully. "It started out with one lady rejecting my suit and ended with another lady in tears at the possibility that *she* might have to marry me."

Cassandra's eyes grew soft and she laid a hand on his arm.

"You mean, you offered for Mrs. Benningham and she turned you down? I am sorry, Christopher. You must be so disappointed."

"Well, naturally, I am disappointed," he said, taken aback.

In truth, he could only feel relieved—if a bit foolish—that Mrs. Benningham had decided she would really rather not be is wife, but he could hardly say so after offering for her. It would only sound like sour grapes.

"I can quite see that the thought of marrying someone else must be extremely distasteful to you right now," she said.

She smiled at him, but it was not a happy smile.

Cassie had a tender heart. Whoever would have thought it? Christopher had a sudden, almost overpowering urge to hold her.

Wouldn't *that* be fun? Ending the day with Cassandra struggling in his arms and screeching the house down.

"Hardly distasteful," he said with perfect truth. Indeed, suddenly the thought of marrying Cassandra was not distasteful at all.

Poor girl.

"Lord Whitby," she said, looking down at their joined hands, "has been most particular in his attentions."

"I have noticed," he said dryly. So, that was it. She was in love with Whitby and she wanted to marry him.

Well, this was hardly a surprise. The curst fellow had been sitting in her pocket for weeks. Christopher had the utmost respect for Cassandra's intelligence—although he could hardly tell *her* that—but she wouldn't be the first girl to have her head turned by the attentions of a good-looking man with a title and expectations of making her a countess when he came into his birthright.

"He has been everything that is kind," Cassandra said carefully. She still couldn't seem to look Christopher in the eye. "He and his parents have procured invitations to a state dinner honoring the tsar and his sister, and they have asked me to accompany them. Just me, without Lady Mayville or Lord Adderly."

"A signal honor," Christopher commented. He understood completely what Cassandra was trying to tell him. If Cassandra appeared at such a function with Lord Whitby and his parents, it was tantamount to a declaration, for all of society would perceive Cassandra as the earl and countess's choice of a bride for their son.

The sweet girl was trying to tell him tactfully that she had made her choice, too. Christopher had never claimed to love her. Indeed, he had never claimed to like her. But she no doubt thought he, along with his grandfather, had his eye on her fortune, her lands, and her father's prize herd of Hereford cows.

"Say no more," Christopher said, forcing himself to smile. He put one hand against her soft lips to stop her from going on. This was difficult for her, and, besides, he would rather be spared her girlish rapture about Lord Whitby. There was something about the fellow he could not like, but he could hardly say so without sounding like a jealous gudgeon and distressing Cassandra further.

"You owe no explanation to me," he said. "You may marry your Lord Whitby with my goodwill, if you want him. In fact, I will put in a good word with Grandfather, if I ever find myself out of his black books."

He released her hands and stood up.

"I must go now," he said ruefully. "I think I have caused enough distress to the members of this household today."

"Christopher—"

She still looked distressed.

He gently touched her damp cheek.

"Do not worry," he assured her. "All will be well."

Then he got out of the house before he did something unforgivable, like kiss all her tears away.

Once he was outside he gave a long sigh of relief.

Whatever had come over him?

He had wanted to kiss *Cassandra*! He had wanted to take her in his arms and never let her go.

He must be going mad.

Eleven

It was an amazing coup to have invitations to the Peace Celebration dinner the Prince Regent would hold in honor of the Tsar of Russia and the King of Prussia at Carlton House the following night, and so Lady Mayville was shocked when Cassandra announced her intention of declining Lord Whitby's request for her to attend the event with him and his parents.

Indeed, Cassandra was perishing to go. She had heard marvelous things about Carlton House, the Prince Regent's private residence, and its splendid decor. Being seen at the dinner would be a social triumph of dizzying proportions, as Lady Mayville was quick to point out.

Everyone would be there. She would have a front row seat at one of the premier entertainments of the Peace Celebrations. She would see the royals tricked out in all their splendid regalia.

She would see the arrogant Duchess of Oldenburg in person and possibly be a witness to some of the outrageous behavior that had all of London engaged in gossip. Indeed, the fascination with the tsar's sister was so great that crowds of gawkers followed her everywhere and London shopkeepers locked their doors and joined the throng with their customers. At one dinner hosted by the Prince Regent soon after the duchess's arrival in March, she annoyed her royal host mightily by demanding that he send away the band engaged for the company's entertainment. She insisted that music made her nauseous.

But if Cassandra accepted Lord Whitby's invitation, she might as well declare to society that she was his for the asking, and she was too unsure about her feelings for the gentleman to commit herself in this way.

"You must be mad to even *think* of refusing," Lady Mayville said as she threw her hands up in exasperation.

"On the contrary, the girl is showing rare good sense," Lord Adderly huffed. "She doesn't want to commit herself to the fellow until she has considered all the alternatives."

The alternative he had in mind, of course, was Christopher.

The last thing she wanted to do was raise *that* expectation in her guardian's breast.

Had she not promised Christopher faithfully that she would resist Lord Adderly's manipulative efforts to force his grandson to the altar with her? He didn't want her. He had made that perfectly plain that day when he had come here at Lord Adderly's demand to receive a tremendous scold for making a spectacle of himself in the park with Mrs. Benningham.

Christopher was in love with the beautiful widow. How could he not be? Compared with her, Cassandra must seem as dull as ditch water. The thought should have cheered her. After all, wasn't marriage to her guardian's grandson a catastrophe she had sought to avoid since she was eleven years old?

Instead, the thought of Christopher marrying another woman depressed her spirits, but she hadn't the leisure for self-examination. Lady Mayville and Lord Adderly were waiting for an explanation for her reluctance to accept an extremely flattering invitation from a handsome and eligible bachelor who would bring his lucky bride a title and the entrée to the highest circles of London society.

Indeed, the invitation to this state dinner was an eloquent demonstration of the earl and countess's influence, therefore their son's, in the polite world.

What Cassandra needed now was to invoke an insuperable obstacle that would excuse her from going to the dinner with Lord Whitby and raising his expectations that she was his for the asking, yet avoid planting the hope in Lord Adderly's breast that she had any intention of marrying his grandson.

Inspiration struck!

"The dinner is tomorrow, and I haven't a thing to wear," she said.

There. That should do it.

"Haven't a thing to wear?" Lord Adderly raved. "Haven't a thing to wear? How, then, do you explain the deskful of dressmaker's bills that have been sent to this house for payment from that highway robber, Miss Lacey?"

Lady Mayville knew exactly what she meant.

"All of your gowns have been seen at one time or another," she said, brow puckering. "How vastly unfortunate."

If she ever expected to hold her head up in society again, Cassandra *could* not wear a gown to the all-important dinner that had been worn at some previous function. It would be *fatal* if someone recognized it. All the other ladies, no doubt, had planned their costumes for this grand occasion weeks ago. Cassandra would be the only one at the dinner in a previously worn gown. Hereafter, when her name was mentioned, someone was sure to recall that she had insulted the Prince Regent before the tsar and embarrassed her escort by appearing in what all would perceive as an old gown, even though it may have left the hands of the dressmaker only ten days ago.

"There's an end to the matter, then. You are quite right, Cassandra. It is out of the question for you to attend," Lady Mayville said in sad resignation. "How extremely unfortunate, because there is no way on earth Miss Lacey could create a new gown for you by tomorrow evening. I suppose we should place an order with Miss Lacey at once for two more gowns so we will be prepared if another invitation is forthcoming."

"Two more gowns!" shouted Lord Adderly. "Do you have any idea what the ones the chit already has have cost me? Absolutely not! I *forbid* you two chuckle-headed females to spend one more groat of my money in that Miss Lacey's shop!"

At that moment, Christopher strolled into the room and looked from Lady Mayville's disappointed face to his grandfather's furious one.

Cassandra had an expression on her face that suggested butter wouldn't melt in her mouth.

The chit was up to something.

Christopher had to grin. Who would have thought the Season would prove so entertaining? Watching the action at Gentleman Jackson's boxing salon was tame sport compared to watching Lady Mayville and Lord Adderly go at it.

He snabbled a biscuit from the tray, sat down on the sofa, and prepared to enjoy the show, thankful that for once it was not *his* head being given over for washing.

Cassandra quietly walked over and sat down beside him on the sofa. He handed her the plate of biscuits and she nibbled delicately at one. A crumb clung to her lower lip.

Christopher had a nearly overwhelming desire to taste it. Hastily, he shook that thought off and leaned forward confidentially.

"What have you done now?" he whispered.

"Nothing. Nothing at all," she said with a smug look on her face that reminded him strongly of hunter cats and feathers.

His aunt and grandfather became aware of him at the same instant.

"Christopher," Lady Mayville said in greeting. Her face lit up in welcome. She apparently considered him some sort of ally in whatever argument was taking place. "Your grandfather is being most unreasonable in the matter of Cassandra's wardrobe."

"Unreasonable! *I* am being unreasonable?" Lord Adderly said. It said something for the state of his agitation that he sought to win Christopher to his side. "The chit has half a dozen gowns already! The two of you act as if I have been clothing her out of the parish poor box."

"She cannot keep wearing the same gowns over and over! It will convey a very *off* impression, I assure you."

Christopher took another biscuit.

"And Cassandra can hardly appear naked in public," he remarked. "That would create an even worse impression."

"Thank you so much for *that* sage observation," Cassandra said dampeningly.

He gave a mocking little nod of his head and pointed to the teapot. Cassandra rolled her eyes and poured him a cup.

"Christopher, I do not believe you understand what is at stake," Lady Mayville said.

"No, I believe I do not," he agreed, smiling at her. "Perhaps you would like to explain it to me."

"Do not bother," Cassandra said dryly. "Men are hopeless in such matters."

"I will have you know, my dear Cassandra, that I am considered quite the expert on matters of feminine adornment," Christopher said. "Be still, now. You are interrupting Aunt Belle."

"Cassandra has received a most flattering invitation from Lord Whitby and his parents to accompany them to the dinner at Carlton House."

"So she tells me. Congratulations, old girl," he said to Cassandra.

"But she cannot attend," Lady Mayville continued, "because all of her gowns have been seen. So we must have new ones made up immediately."

"That is the most preposterous and wasteful thing I have ever heard," Lord Adderly grumbled.

"What about the green thing she was trying on at Miss Lacey's?" Christopher asked, taking another biscuit. "I haven't seen her wear that yet."

He waggled his eyebrows suggestively.

"I would have remembered *that*!"

Cassandra turned fierce eyes upon Christopher and struck him on the arm.

"Ow! What was *that* for!" he exclaimed, rubbing his afflicted limb. It *hurt*! Who would think a little thing like Cassandra could hit so hard?

Lady Mayville gasped.

"You are right!" she cried excitedly. "Cassandra *hasn't* worn the sea green gauze yet, and it is quite one of her most expensive gowns. I don't know how we could have forgotten it. It will be *perfect*! My dear boy, I cannot thank you enough!"

She ran over to the sofa and kissed Christopher on both cheeks.

"There, then," Lord Adderly said, looking pleased

with Christopher for once. "The matter is solved. Cassandra will wear *that* to her precious dinner tomorrow night. The boy just saved me a fortune."

"Not so fast, Jasper," Lady Mayville said, pursuing the gentleman purposefully when he walked through the doorway. "That does not answer the matter of the two gowns we must have made for Cassandra without delay in the event that she receives an invitation to some other state event!"

"Thunderation!" the viscount's voice boomed from the hall. "Will you give me no peace?"

Christopher heard the viscount's heavy stomped footsteps retreat down the hall followed by Lady Mayville's lighter, more staccato ones. She apparently was trotting briskly after him to keep up.

"I am not finished talking to you, Jasper," the lady's voice called. She sounded a bit breathless. "Stop at *once!*"

Smiling, Christopher turned to Cassandra in expectation of sharing his amusement. His smile faded. Cassandra looked as if she would like to hit him again.

"You *had* to remember that stupid gown," she said accusingly. "Why can you never mind your own business?"

His mouth dropped open in surprise.

"Ungrateful chit! I should think you would be ready to kiss me for making it possible for you to accept the invitation of the Season. Instead, you practically maim me."

"Kiss you! Hardly," she scoffed as if he were the most loathsome beast in creation.

"You have no idea how relieved I am to hear it," he said, scowling at her. "Now you can go to the dinner with Lord Whitby and let him drool down your décolletage. It is what you wanted all the time, is it not? To drive the silly gudgeon mad with passion for you?"

Christopher would consent to be flogged before he admitted how much he would like to be in Lord Whitby's shoes.

"You know nothing about the matter," she grumped.

"What is this?" he asked, reaching out to place a hand under her chin and raise her face so she had no choice but to look at him. She struck his hand away. She looked genuinely vexed. "I thought your Lord Whitby was the answer to all your maidenly prayers. Am I to assume your idol has feet of clay, and you do not wish to marry him after all?" The thought delighted him. "Am I to quake in my boots?"

Instead of coaxing a smile from her, as he intended, these words only seemed to make her defensive.

What the deuce?

Cassandra's skin seemed to burn where he touched it, which filled her with confusion. Since when did the touch of the bane of her childhood set her skin to tingling?

Since *never*, she told herself firmly.

How he would recoil with horror if he knew that his face, and not Lord Whitby's, filled her dreams at night.

"You needn't worry. I wouldn't have you if you were the last man on earth," she lied in order to save her pride.

"Then why did you look at me as if you would cheerfully cut out my heart when I—"

He broke off and narrowed his eyes at her. Then he burst out laughing.

"You sly little minx," he said. "What a cloth head I am!"

"Now, *that* is something upon which we may agree," she said stiffly.

"You and my aunt have put your heads together to see how you could inveigle my grandfather into permitting you to purchase more new gowns. No wonder you wish me to the devil for spoiling sport by remembering the green one." He seemed pleased with himself for coming up with this explanation for her irrational behavior. "I am sorry, Cassie. I truly did not mean to cheat you out of some new finery. I know how important it is for females to be slap up to the echo on grand occasions."

Well! He made her sound like the most manipulative of schemers. However, that was infinitely preferable to having him guess the truth—that she was not so sure, after all, that she wished to marry Lord Whitby.

Lord Whitby was everything a lady could want in a husband. This sudden infatuation she had with Christopher must be a symptom of bridal nerves. It was said this ailment could quite rob a girl of rational thought, and now Cassandra had no trouble believing it.

She knew exactly whom to thank for Christopher's newly acquired knowledge of females. The beautiful and accommodating Mrs. Benningham, of course.

"Exactly so," she said. "A girl cannot have too many evening gowns."

"Greedy, are we?" he asked tolerantly. "Fair enough. Good luck in persuading Grandfather to waste more of the ready on new gowns. If you ask my opinion, that sea green one is *much* too good for old Whitby."

Cassandra blinked.

He sounded almost . . . jealous.

But he was only teasing again.

"I *never* ask your opinion about anything truly important, Christopher," she said archly, "do have the last biscuit. You've already had all the others."

"Thank you, I will," he said. "It is obvious that my aunt and grandfather are in no humor to talk to me, and I've already worn out my welcome with you, so I'll be on my way."

With that, he stuffed the last biscuit in his mouth, made her an elaborately mocking bow and sauntered from the room.

No heroine of a romance could have asked for a better setting than Carlton House. Despite her best intentions, Cassandra could not maintain the character of a blasé young woman of the world when she and the rest of the earl's party were admitted into the double doors of Carlton House to enter a vast apartment full of shields emblazoned with the quarterings of England and a profusion of elaborate crystal chandeliers suspended from carved monastic heads.

Through a wide open Gothic door she could see out into the gardens and a dramatic landscape of weeping willows, live peacocks strutting on the grounds and brightly colored lanterns suspended on poles to rival the brilliance of the sun.

"It is all so vulgar, is it not?" Lord Whitby observed with tolerant good humor as he leaned close to whisper in her ear.

She looked at him in surprise.

Vulgar? She thought it was *wonderful.*

He laughed and tapped the tip of her nose with a careless forefinger as if she were a child, and not a particularly precocious one at that.

"Such an adorable innocent," he whispered. "It is all quite overpowering, isn't it?"

Disgruntled, Cassandra longed to tell him that she was not overpowered in the least, and she wanted to go back to the rest of the company now. The guests had been strolling through the prince's art-filled apartments before dinner, and although she found the lovely treasures from Versailles that the prince had bought at public auction after the French Revolution fascinating, she was a bit tired of being patronized by Lord Whitby, who took it upon himself to explain everything she was seeing to her as if she hadn't eyes of her own. Or a *mind* of her own to form an opinion.

He was much too close. He had not let her out of his sight from the moment she walked through the door. He did, however, make her known to several of his parents' intimates. And the earl and countess were perfectly polite to her in their usual chilly way. The countess had even referred to her once or twice as she performed introductions as "our Cassandra."

She supposed she should feel gratified, but it only made her feel trapped. Her face must have mirrored her discomfort, for Whitby leaned close again.

"You look charming," he said. "There is no reason to feel self-conscious."

"I am not self-conscious," she replied.

"That's the spirit, my dear," he said in approval.

He thought she was self-conscious about her gown, the sea green gauze that she had once thought so ravishing. Well, he was right about that!

Now it looked quite different thanks to Lady Mayville's helpful suggestions.

Instead of being slightly *décolleté* as it was originally designed, it was made up almost to the throat with a ribbon-trimmed net ruffle around the neckline that itched and, for some peculiar reason, white rosettes of satin. More rosettes and ribbons were threaded through her hair.

Add a crook and a stuffed lamb and she could act the part of a sheperdess at a masquerade. The dress was that sweetly insipid.

She hated it.

Cassandra had not wanted to hurt kind Lady Mayville's feelings by saying so when it arrived from the dressmaker's, however, so she simply allowed it to gather dust in the back of her wardrobe and hoped Lady Mayville would forget all about it.

She would have, too, if it hadn't been for Christopher.

Another thing Cassandra hated was thinking of *him* all the time. She wondered what he would think of Carlton House, for example, and if he was with Mrs. Benningham right this minute.

If he was, she told herself, she was sure she did not give a rap.

To her surprise, Lord Whitby *liked* the dress. It was "sweet" and "charming" and "innocent." He declared that her appearance did him enormous credit. Already his mother loved her like a daughter, he added.

Cassandra repressed a shudder.

"Cold?" he asked solicitiously. He was leaning much too close again, and people were looking at them with benign, knowing smiles on their faces. "Shall I have a footman fetch your wrap?"

"Cold!" she said with a snort before she could stop herself. "Hardly, in this heat."

He must think her the most fragile of hothouse flowers. The prince kept his rooms to a sweltering temperature. One lady had already fainted from the heat and had to be taken out into the gardens to be revived.

"Let us go into the gallery," she suggested.

She had come, after all, to see the Prince Regent and the foreign potentates. Surely they would make an entrance at any moment. So far, Lord Whitby and his parents had not introduced her to anyone particularly interesting.

"As you wish, my pet," Lord Whitby said indulgently. She *hated* it when he called her that. "I suppose it is to be expected that you would want to see the royals. I hope you will not be too disappointed."

He said this for all the world as if seeing kings and princes and generals were an everyday occurrence for him, and the fact that she *did* want to see them no doubt made her seem hopelessly naive.

They went to stand in the long gallery, however, and joined in the applause when the Prince Regent appeared in his field marshal's uniform with an impressive array of foreign orders glittering on a crimson sash across his chest. The unsmiling tsar wore a white uniform, also glittering with orders. And the grand duchess looked proud and conveyed the impression that she thought herself leagues above the greatest nobles and most powerful politicians in England.

Lord Whitby almost spoiled the moment by whispering what he apparently considered witty, irreverent observations in Cassandra's ear about each one.

Did she know that crowds followed the tsar and grand duchess wherever they went? That the grand duchess so abhorred music that she made a scene if her hosts arranged for singers to perform after dinner? That the prince had to control his girth with corsets, and if you listened carefully, you could hear them creak when he bowed?

Of course Cassandra knew these things. She rather

wished he would just be still and let her enjoy the pageantry.

Dinner itself was what one would expect to see in the home of an Epicurean of the Prince Regent's stature.

"No wonder His Highness is so fat," the countess said indulgently. She looked pointedly at Cassandra's full plate.

Cassandra ignored her disapproval and ate every scrumptious bite.

The countess looked at her sadly at the end of the meal after Cassandra had devoured a selection of pastries, creams, and jellies.

Lord Whitby put a casual arm across the back of Cassandra's chair and looked his mother straight in the eye.

"I find it refreshing to find a young woman who enjoys her food," he said. "All healthy young animals do so. It is only natural."

Now Cassandra had degenerated from sweet and charming and innocent to being a healthy young animal. Of course, it fit with "my pet."

Cassandra defiantly tipped the rest of the champagne from her glass down her throat and smiled at the hovering waiter who came to refill it.

Lord Whitby and his mother both looked shocked, and Cassandra gave a small grin of satisfaction. She'd show *them* who was sweet and charming and innocent.

Unfortunately, she dissolved into a fit of the hiccups with the last swallow of her second glass of champagne.

"Edmund, she's inebriated," the countess said disapprovingly.

"Nonsense," Lord Whitby said. "Just a case of the hiccups."

He imperiously signaled the waiter.

"A glass of water for the young lady," he said sternly. "And no more champagne for her."

When Cassandra had gulped down the water, her hiccups abated. Even so, Lord Whitby pulled Cassandra's chair back and extended his arm.

"Come along, my dear. Let us get you into the fresh air," he said, looking pointedly at his outstretched hand.

Since she had already eaten a large meal with a goodly portion of the sweets and no one would give her any more champagne, she accepted it.

He quickly towed her out into the gardens and put his hands on her shoulders.

"Better now?" he asked kindly.

"Lord Whitby," she said with all the dignity she could muster, "there is nothing whatsoever wrong with me."

"Well, it would not be surprising if drinking champagne made you sick or dizzy."

"I am neither sick nor dizzy. I have had champagne before. I am two-and-twenty years old, for heaven's sake!"

He smiled.

"My apologies," he said. "But you can hardly blame me for seizing a perfect opportunity to get you into the gardens alone while the other guests are nodding over their port."

He leaned close, as if he were going to kiss her.

"We should go back inside. We will be missed," she said.

She had no intention of embarking upon a romantic interlude that would commit her irrevocably to this man if they were discovered.

He released her at once and gave her a small, ironic bow.

"You remind me, quite properly, that a gentleman does not trifle with an innocent lady who deserves his utmost respect."

He extended his arm, and Cassandra thought the formal gesture was intended to signal the end of their private interlude. She accepted it with relief.

Before they reached the door, however, he drew her into the dark shadow of a tree and framed her face with his hands.

"Just one kiss to get me through an interminable evening," he said huskily before he forced her mouth open with his lips.

He had been eating smoked fish. She almost gagged.

She pushed her hands against his chest and almost sent him sprawling.

He looked absolutely shocked.

"I don't know you well enough," she said lamely.

Oh, good. Now she was apologizing because *he* had decided to maul her. He must think her a complete ninny.

However, her show of maidenly shrinking served the purpose.

"I am sorry," he said ruefully. "My ardor overcame my good judgment. It frequently does, I fear. Perhaps I am the one who has drunk too much champagne."

"You are forgiven," she said, eager to put an end to this ridiculous scene.

After that, she had tea and refreshments with the ladies while they waited for the gentlemen to join them. The countess was at her most affable and introduced Cassandra to the wives of several powerful men with whom Cassandra had heretofore been acquainted only through reading the newspapers. The grand duchess even condescended to extend two fingers to her.

In Devonshire, she could have dined out on this for years.

Her dazzled eyes drank in every detail of the magnificence that was Carlton House on that perfect June evening, for she knew she would not be returning.

The price of admission was entirely too high if it meant she had to marry Lord Whitby to earn it.

Twelve

It was quite possibly the most embarrassing moment of Christopher's life.

He sat on the edge of Mrs. Benningham's extravagant, gold brocade-draped bed and held his head in his hands.

His chest was bare, and only his pantaloons preserved his modesty. Mrs. Benningham, dressed in a revealing green silk chemise, put her hands on his shoulders and rested her forehead against the back of his neck.

The remains of their intimate supper rested on a nearby table along with an empty bottle of champagne.

Fully recovered at last, Mrs. Benningham had made good on her promise to fulfill his every fantasy. Only, it seemed, Christopher found it impossible to keep up his, er, side of the bargain.

Damnation.

"It happens to everyone sooner or later, Christopher," Mrs. Benningham said soothingly.

"I must have had too much champagne," he lied to save her feelings. Not for the world would he do—or not do—anything to feed her insecurity about her age and attractiveness. "Perhaps in a moment—"

He rather doubted a second attempt would prove more successful, but he owed it to her to try.

Incredibly, she laughed.

"Not *that*, darling. I meant falling in love."

"Falling in love," he repeated blankly.

"Personally, I have not had too much experience with that particular phenomenon, but I have grown somewhat familiar with the symptoms," she said as she traced a swirling pattern on the bare skin of his back.

It should have set him on fire. Instead, it rather tickled.

"I have no idea what you are talking about," he said, glad she couldn't see his face.

"I'm talking about your Cassandra, of course."

He gave a short bark of mirthless laughter.

"Good God, I am not in love with Cassandra!" he said, and wished it were true.

"Your voice changes when you say her name. Did you know that?"

"No. I didn't," he said with a sigh of resignation.

"I do not suppose you have done anything sensible to remedy the situation, such as talk to *her* about it."

"How could I?" he said harshly. "She thinks I am the filthiest beast in nature. And she is in love with Lord Whitby."

"Lord Whitby," Mrs. Benningham repeated.

Christopher's head snapped around at the tone of her voice.

"What is it?" he said as he looked into her eyes. "Your voice changes when you say *his* name, too, did you know?"

She tossed her disheveled dark hair.

"Only from a fit of pique, I assure you," she said with a smile. "Men are such hypocrites." She arched an eyebrow at the expression on his face. "Oh, not *you*, darling. You are quite special in that regard. I think no matter what happens, you will still be my friend."

"You are right," he said, remembering how Lord Whitby had given him and Mrs. Benningham the cut direct that day in the park when he took Cassandra riding and how Cassandra had deliberately refused to ride on without speaking to them.

"You are thinking about her again," Mrs. Benningham said, sounding amused. "I can tell by the expression on your face."

He lowered his eyes and took her hand.

"Caroline—"

She raised her free hand to his lips.

"Lucky, lucky Miss Davies," she said lightly. "I wonder which of you she will choose."

Christopher gave a snort of derision.

"Whitby, of course. Can you doubt it?"

"Well, she would not be the first young girl captivated by a handsome face and a title," Mrs. Benningham said sadly. "Giles was such a man."

She rarely spoke of her late husband. Christopher gathered he had used her very badly.

"Lord Whitby is hardly the rotter Giles was," she said when Christopher pressed her hand.

"Stop trying to cheer me up," Christopher said sardonically.

"That does not mean she will choose him," Mrs. Benningham said.

"Yes, she will," he said glumly. "He can give her everything she wants."

Mrs. Benningham walked her fingers up Christopher's bare chest.

"Such a waste," she said with a sigh. "However . . . do you care for a game of cards?"

He smiled.

"Why not?"

It was still relatively early when Lord Whitby and his parents took Cassandra home. So early, in fact, that Lord Adderly and Lady Mayville were still up.

"There's our girl," Lady Mayville crowed when Lord Whitby ushered her inside. "But why have you come home so early?"

"Someone had a bit too much champagne," Whitby said archly.

Cassandra forced herself to smile for Lady Mayville's sake, although she wanted to grit her teeth.

"Naughty me," she said.

She had *not* drunk too much champagne. She was perfectly fine. Yet Lord Whitby and his parents insisted upon taking her home early because she was a "trifle indisposed."

Not that her escort had uttered a single word of reproach.

On the contrary, he apparently thought it endearing that two glasses of champagne could be too much for her.

"You will feel better in the morning, my dear," he said solicitously.

"I feel quite all right now," she could not stop herself from saying, even though it would do little good.

At least she was permitted to enjoy some of the conversation in the drawing room before Lord Whitby and his parents swept her out of Carlton House, no doubt for fear that she would embark upon some drunken rambling or knock over a teacup and disgrace them.

He patted her cheek as if she were a child and took his leave.

"Do you feel well enough to tell us about your evening, my dear, or would you rather go straight to bed?" Lady Mayville asked.

"I am not in the least sleepy," Cassandra said, knowing that she sounded peevish. "And I would be delighted to tell you all about it. First of all, Carlton Place is the most *sumptuous* house I have ever seen. The prince has one whole room dedicated to art from Versailles, and—"

At that moment, Christopher entered the room and stopped dead in surprise at seeing her.

He had drunk just enough at Mrs. Benningham's house to take the edge off his anxiety, but not nearly enough to erase the humiliation he had suffered in failing to exercise his manly prowess on a lady who was generally acknowledged to be the most alluring in London. They had played a hand or two of cards, and he had left as soon as he could without giving offense.

It was early yet, but he had no taste for drinking and gaming with his male acquaintances. How could he, with his recent disgrace on his mind? What if liquor loosened his tongue and he blurted the horrible truth out to them?

If that happened, he might as well be dead.

Yet he could not bring himself to go back to his solitary lodgings; the last thing he wanted was to be alone. The thought that he might be in love with Cassandra was too new. Too disconcerting.

Maybe it wasn't that at all. Maybe he simply had lost the ability to perform with any woman after his imprisonment in France. It is true he had not been with a woman since then. He had no taste for visiting brothels, and he spent most of the time he wasn't squiring Mrs. Benningham about town boxing at Gentleman Jackson's, fencing at Angelo's, or riding his horse in the park.

These manly pursuits had a way of exorcising his sexual frustrations.

It never occurred to him that he might be *incapable* of making love to a woman. Perhaps he had contracted some debilitating disease along with prison fever at Bitche or Valenciennes. He had suffered from the malady in both places.

This thought was only slightly more alarming than the possibility that he genuinely might be in love with Cassandra.

There was a lost cause!

So, here he was. In his aunt's parlor, spoiling for a fight.

If there was anyone on earth who might be depended upon to give it to him, it was his grandfather.

Finding Cassandra at home was just a bonus.

The thought that he might be in love with the bossy little baggage was preposterous, he told himself. Simply preposterous.

"Look who is back from Carlton House," he observed.

Good. He would pick a fight with her, too. *That* should lay to rest the ridiculous notion that he might be in love with her.

She had a mulish expression on her face.

He grinned, knowing it would annoy her.

Then he cocked his head in puzzlement and got out the quizzing glass. He walked all around her as she clenched her fists in anger.

"What happened to it?" he asked. The last time he had seen the sea green gauze ball gown, it had fit her like a glove and made the most of a slender, ripening figure.

Now it had this fussy filmy stuff all over the neckline trimmed with artificial white flowers that looked like nothing in nature. More filmy stuff had been sewn around the hem caught up in places with more of the white flowers.

It looked silly—*she* looked silly—and he was feeling mean enough to tell her so.

"It was far too low at the bosom," Lady Mayville explained. "Cassandra could hardly wear a gown like that in public. What would people think? An unmarried girl must convey every impression of propriety."

"Lord, if it isn't just like a woman," he said scornfully, "to take something simple and honest and put a lot of gewgaws on it. I suppose your precious Lord Whitby likes it this way."

"You are offensive, sir!" said Lord Adderly.

"As a matter of fact, he does," Cassandra snapped at the same time.

"And Cassandra looks lovely," Lady Mayville said.

"Hah! She looks like a day-old pastry. One of those Bavarian ones filled with lukewarm custard and so much sugar icing it makes your teeth hurt to bite into one," Christopher said with a mirthless laugh. "And all to hide a bit of bosom."

"My bosom is absolutely none of your business, Christopher Warrender, for which I thank the Almighty every day of my life," Cassandra shouted.

"Cassandra!" wailed Lady Mayville, absolutely scandalized.

"Not half so often as I do," Christopher shouted back. He looked over his shoulder at Lord Adderly. "And I want you to increase my allowance."

"The devil I will," fumed Lord Adderly, rising at once to the bait. "I have half a mind to cut it off entirely after this performance!"

"I refuse to stay here a moment longer and listen to this," Lady Mayville said with great dignity as she rose and gathered the embroidery she had been working on. "I am going to bed."

Silence reigned until she had left the room.

"I know what it is," Lord Adderly said to Christopher. "You are drunk! You can either go to your lodgings and sleep off your excesses or find somewhere else to sleep here. But you will present yourself here tomorrow, for you and I have many things to discuss."

He stalked to the door, but then stopped and looked back at Cassandra.

"You should go to bed, too, girl," he said in a gentler tone. "Champagne will give you the devil of a head if you are not accustomed to it."

Then he left them alone.

Cassandra put her hands on her hips.

Well, he had come here for a fight, and it looked like she, at least, was of a mood to indulge him.

"So, you've been drinking deep of the grape, have you?" he said. "Did that fellow Whitby try to get you tipsy so he could lead you out to the gardens at Carlton Place and grope you in the dark?"

She didn't reply. She didn't need to. The look on her face told him that he had guessed correctly.

Damn and blast! Christopher could feel himself growing fangs.

"Lord Whitby," Cassandra said carefully, "has been all that is gentlemanly."

"You are lying," he said. "You never did learn the way of it."

"He is in love with me," she said, not meeting his eyes. "He wants to marry me."

"Good for him," he said sarcastically. "And what about you? Do you want to marry him?"

She just looked at him with that obstinate look on her face.

"Of course, you do," he said, scornfully answering his own question. "Lord Whitby is what you and all the silly little debutantes want."

"You know nothing about me!" she shouted.

"Oh, I think I do," he said mockingly. "I have no doubt that you may be able to support the character of a demure, properly submissive little ingenue until you get the fellow's ring on your finger, but do you think you can keep a guard on your sharp tongue and independent nature for *years*?"

He grasped her shoulders, and Cassandra turned her face away from him.

She did not want to hear it.

Well, that was too damned bad!

"Living like that will kill you!" he shouted. "You'll turn into a juiceless, dried-up old prune, saying 'yes, Edmund,' and 'as you please, Edmund,' all the day long. Look at his parents! Do you want to be bloodless shells, like them?"

"Get . . . your . . . hands . . . *off* me," she said through gritted teeth, but her eyes were full of tears.

"Damn it, Cassandra! I can't let you do it!" he declared, and crushed her slim body against his chest.

Cassandra's head was spinning. Maybe Lord Whitby had been right. Maybe she had drunk too much champagne, after all.

Her heart was beating so hard and fast that she feared it would leap from her chest altogether. But that was all right because, incredibly, through her thin gown and fine muslin chemise pressed so close to Christopher's chest, she could feel his heart beating just as fast as hers.

It didn't occur to her to fight *him* off.

The look in his wonderful hazel eyes was so compelling that she had no choice but to raise her face and watch those eyes catch fire as he covered her mouth his.

She tasted hunger and champagne and something fruity like strawberries.

Delicious.

He didn't hold her as if she were a precious piece of porcelain that might shatter into a hundred pieces with rough handling. Instead, he grasped her possessively, as if he would never let her go. She might have bruises in the morning, but she didn't care.

His lips were demanding, and she had no choice but to give.

When his mouth forced hers to open, she gave him access without hesitation. Her arms went around his shoulders and clung. He made a small satisfied growl deep in his throat and feasted on her.

Her hunger equaled his and soon her tongue was probing *his* mouth with equal intensity. She could not get enough of him.

Abruptly, he let go of her and stepped back. He covered his mouth with his hands.

"I'm going to be sick," he announced, looking at her with anguish in his eyes.

He had released her so quickly that she stumbled and had to catch herself by grasping the back of a chair.

It *nauseated* him to kiss her, just as it nauseated Cassandra when Lord Whitby used his tongue on her. She had never been so insulted and so hurt in her entire life. She wanted to die.

No. She wanted *him* to die.

"I think," she said, scrubbing her lips with one gloved hand, "that you are the most disgusting man who ever lived."

"I am sorry," he said, breathing hard. "It is not your fault. I had too much to drink tonight. It will not happen again, I promise you."

Champagne. Strawberries.

Of course. How could she have been such a fool?

While she had been wrapped in his arms, her senses had been filled with an exotic, musky fragrance.

"You have been with *her*, haven't you?" she demanded. "*Haven't* you!"

"A gentleman . . . doesn't kiss and tell," he muttered. He gulped alarmingly.

"Don't you *dare* vomit in here, you vile creature!"

"No . . . I didn't . . . with her. I . . . couldn't," he gasped. He lurched toward her with one hand extended in appeal.

Cassandra, watching the way his Adam's apple bobbed, twitched her skirts back to protect them from the inevitable.

"Do not bother to lie to me," she snarled. "You reek of her perfume."

He recoiled.

"Were you thinking of *her* when you kissed me?" she demanded.

"No," he said, taking deep breaths. He gave her a rueful smile, even though his face was still a little green. "The crisis is over. I think the contents of my stomach have settled now."

She did not believe either statement.

He still looked as if he were going to be sick. His face was shiny with perspiration.

And he *had* been thinking of Caroline Benningham, and not Cassandra, when he was kissing her. Otherwise, why did he get sick to his stomach when he opened his eyes to look at her?

The blackguard! With one careless act he had *ruined* her for all other men.

"I hate you!" she cried. "I *hate* you!"

A red haze clouded her vision, and of its own volition, her hand swung in an arc and struck him hard across the face.

She gasped and covered her mouth with both hands.

What had she done?

They stared into one another's eyes, appalled, for a moment.

Then he gave her a rueful smile. The effect was devastating, even though he still looked a trifle green around the edges.

"Well, that makes two of us," he said calmly.

"I apologize," she said. "I should not have done that."

"You have every right." He sank to the sofa and buried his head in his hands. "I have behaved abominably."

"Yes, you have," she agreed, but she put one hand on his shoulder in concern. "You truly are not well, are you?"

"I am drunk," he said baldly. "Can you doubt it after the way I . . . Bloody hell! The whole room is spinning."

He fell back against the cushions and looked up at the ceiling.

"I have made a proper fool of myself, have I not?" he said bitterly. "I had better go while I still have some pride left."

Cassandra put her hands on his shoulders to keep him down when he would have risen to his feet. It said something for his physical condition that he merely sagged back against the cushions.

"No harm done," she said, struggling to sound matter-of-fact. "Fortunately, you only made a fool of your-self in front of me, and I always knew you were an ass."

"Oh, that is *most* comforting," he said with an abrupt laugh. "Let me up. I must go."

"No. There are no hackney carriages in the neighborhood, and I can hardly rouse the coachman at this hour to take you home."

"I came on horseback. I can leave the same way."

"In your condition? You will break your neck," she said scornfully.

He gave a long sigh.

"You are probably right," he admitted.

"I will help you up to one of the bedrooms," she said, taking his hand.

"I do not think I can make it," he said, smiling wanly. "I will just sleep here."

He flopped back on the sofa and covered his eyes with his hands.

"Are you sure?" she asked doubtfully. The sofa was at least a foot shorter than he was. "It will be most uncomfortable."

He gave another of those short, bitter laughs of self-mockery.

"I have slept in worse places," he said.

Of course. He had been held hostage in some of the worst prisons in France.

"Very well," she said.

"What are you doing?" he said in alarm when she knelt and began to remove one of his shoes. They were made of black butter-soft leather, of the kind designed for ballroom dancing.

"You will be all right," she said soothingly as she removed the other shoe. "Just try to go to sleep."

Cassandra stepped away and looked down at him, lying there with his hair mussed and his eyes rimmed with red. Blast him! His face was pale and sheened with perspiration, but he still looked rakishly handsome in his rumpled evening clothes and his snowy linen.

His eyes closed, as if he could not bear to look at her.

She moved to the lamp and was about to extinguish it, but his voice stopped her.

"Leave it on," he said. His voice broke. "Please, Cassandra. I have spent far too much time in solitary confinement to find comfort in the dark."

Her heart melted.

She left the room, but she soon came back with a coverlet from her own bed. Christopher, poor man, appeared to be asleep, so she tucked it carefully around him and then, with a slight hesitation, she kissed his damp forehead.

He will never know, she told herself.

Thirteen

Christopher awoke with the devil's own head.

Every bone in his body ached.

His mouth was full of cotton wool.

Gingerly, he raised himself to a sitting position, and a light sprig muslin coverlet slid from his shoulders. A wisp of fresh, clean lavender scent clung to it. It smelled like *her*.

Then he remembered.

Cassandra had covered him with this. He had felt her lips touch his brow, as if he had been a weary little boy and she had been his nurse.

He had been such a pathetic mess last night she didn't even trust him to ride home. He had reacted like an outraged virgin when she removed his shoes to keep him from sullying his aunt's brocade sofa.

That was *after* he lost his head and thrust his tongue halfway down the poor girl's throat.

She should have thrown him into the street. It would have been kinder.

How could he face her?

How could he face *either* of them, for he had made a fool of himself in front of two women last night.

With Mrs. Benningham, he could not function.

With Cassandra, his traitorous body could have functioned all too well.

God! The way she tasted. The way she smelled. The way she felt in his arms.

She hated him. Really hated him.

She slapped him hard enough to make his ears ring.

And who could blame her?

He had been drunk, he told himself firmly.

Simply drunk out of his mind.

He was *not* in love with Cassandra. If he kissed her again, nothing would happen.

Absolutely nothing.

Then she walked in the room with a cup of tea in her hand, and he felt every muscle in his body—even *that* one—spring to attention.

Curse it all!

"Here you are, Christopher," Cassandra said, placing the teacup and saucer on the table at his elbow. She was wearing a light blue muslin gown that left her pretty arms bare. Her hair was tied up in a simple style with a matching ribbon.

He couldn't take his eyes off her.

"Why are you looking at me like that?" she asked in sudden alarm. "See here, you are not going to be sick, are you?"

"No, of course not," he said, closing his eyes in the hope that when he opened them again she would merely look like Cassie, the irritating chit who had plagued his youth, instead of the most desirable woman he had ever seen in his life. He opened his eyes again.

No such luck.

He still wanted very badly to kiss her, and he knew she *would* slap him silly this time.

He rose creakily to his feet with the cup of tea cradled in both hands and drank it straight down.

"If you're wise, you'll ride home now before your grandfather catches you," she said warningly. "What were you about, riding about town on horseback in your evening clothes? At least it's too early for anyone to see you leave the house."

"Ah, so *that* is why you are suddenly so solicitous," he said. "You just want to be rid of me. I should have known."

"I do not know what you mean," she replied. Her brow was furrowed a bit in confusion and he wanted to smooth out those little furrows and kiss her closed eyelids.

He must be mad. Or still drunk. That was the more palatable explanation.

"Wouldn't it be terrible if it came to Whitby's ears that I had left the house at an unseasonably early hour of the morning in evening dress and looking as if I'd had the ride of my life. He might think—perish forbid—that his demure little damsel is human."

"He would think," Cassandra said, hands on hips, "that you had lost your mind."

Well, that would be two of them, he thought ruefully.

"I'll go," he said. "Here. You'll need this to keep you warm. Old Whitby is hardly the man to do the job."

He handed her the coverlet and stalked to the door with every shred of dignity he could muster.

"Christopher!" she called after him.

He turned.

"Yes?"

"You might want to take your shoes," she said.

"Oh. Yes."

So much for dignity.

* * *

Cassandra had not wanted to come, but if she hadn't, it would have been an admission of error.

She would be flogged before she admitted to Christopher that Lord Whitby was not the man for her, just as he had told her all along, after she had declared so passionately that he knew nothing about her heart.

The occasion was a grand party at the home of Lord Whitby's parents to celebrate their wedding anniversary.

She didn't wear the sea green dress. She never wanted to see the wretched thing again. Instead she wore the white gown, and because it was so simple, she instructed her maid to dress her hair in a profusion of ringlets threaded with white ribbon.

When she looked in the mirror, she thought the simple Grecian lines made her look like a virgin sacrifice.

"Are you all right?" Lord Whitby asked solicitously when she declined a second serving of one of her favorite dishes.

Lord Whitby might be impervious to anything but his own self-consequence, but even he had noticed that, as a rule, Cassandra had a healthy appetite. And disapproved, no doubt. Well, *this* should make him happy.

"I am not very hungry tonight," she said.

He smiled at her.

"It is the excitement, of course," he said indulgently.

Naturally he would expect a countrified young lady to be overset by the spectacle of twenty couples at a dining room table.

Oh, it was all very grand, but it was also very tedious. Lord Whitby's parents, for all the elegant appointments of their parties, were so staid and dignified that no one with any dash ever attended. Either the earl and countess did not invite them or, if they did, the prospective guests were quick to decline in the certain knowledge they would be bored to tears by the time the second course was served.

Later there would be music, and Cassandra would be asked to perform as Lady Mayville looked on proudly. At his sister's side, Lord Adderly looked as if he had indigestion, as well he might. It was precisely the sort of event he hated.

Mercifully, the evening would end relatively soon by London standards. As a rule, the earl and countess preferred to retire early.

Lady Mayville and Lord Adderly were seated at some distance from Cassandra, which made her feel even more strongly that she was here under false pretenses. She had been placed close to the head of the table next to Lord Whitby, who had introduced her to all the more prominent guests present before dinner. She had noticed several sly looks directed her way from some of the ladies, which made her want to sink.

Oh, to be a man!

Christopher, she was sure, would never find himself at such a dull party. Men could go anywhere. They did not have to wait to be invited.

More importantly, men could marry anyone they wished. They did not have to wait to be asked.

Cassandra told herself that all she needed to do was get through the evening. She could even pretend to have a headache so that she could ask her guardian to take her home unobtrusively as soon as the ladies left the gentlemen to their port, even though she disliked the idea of reinforcing Lord Whitby's nonsensical belief that all well-bred young ladies were frail flowers who became overset at the least excitement. Tonight his misapprehension of her nature would work in her favor.

From down the table, Lady Mayville gave Cassandra a questioning look. Cassandra didn't doubt she had noticed Cassandra's discomfort and was puzzled by it. Bless her heart. Cassandra had found in her guardian's sister a formidable ally, for she had made a love match years ago and was determined to help Cassandra do the same. She was even prepared to brave the wrath of her brother to do so.

Unfortunately, though, Lady Mayville had been misguided into thinking that Cassandra was head over heels in love with Lord Whitby. This was Cassandra's fault entirely for rhapsodizing upon the handsome and attentive Lord Whitby's perfections early in their acquaintance. It was no wonder that Lady Mayville assumed that Cassandra's new reserve toward Lord Whitby was nothing but maidenly coyness.

Cassandra would have to take her into her confidence as soon as possible. Lady Mayville would be disappointed that Cassandra was not about to make a romantic love match with an earl's son, but she would understand when Cassandra explained that she could never care for him in that way.

Explaining *why* would be the challenge. Any young lady in her right mind would be over the moon at the prospect of marrying Lord Whitby.

Of course, Cassandra was *not* in her right mind. All she could think about was that wonderful kiss she had shared with Christopher last night.

It was an aberration. It had to be.

If she kissed him again, it would not be the same.

Her thoughts were interrupted when Lord Whitby clasped her hand under the table and squeezed it.

She jumped, startled by his breath on her cheek.

"Thinking of me?" he said warmly. "You had the dreamiest expression on your face."

She blushed crimson. She could not help it. But it would have been extremely impolite to tell him that she had forgotten his very existence while she relived Christopher's kiss.

He was so sure of her that he wouldn't have believed her, anyway.

"Actually, it was the buttered peas," she said, making a joke of it. "I am extremely fond of a dish of buttered peas."

He laughed, not a whit insulted. Naturally it would not occur to him that he was not the answer to her most ardent prayers.

How odd that Lady Mayville had noticed her reticence when it came to Lord Whitby, but the gentleman himself had not the least notion that anything was lacking in her feelings toward him.

This was just one more reason why she had to tell him, as soon as possible, that they would not suit.

Once she had made this decision, the knots in her stomach relaxed as if by magic.

She would invent that headache when the ladies rose from the table, she decided. All she had to do now was get through the meal.

It was the last social invitation she would accept from Lord Whitby under false pretenses. Then she would be free.

She looked up with a smile when the earl stood and raised his glass. He signaled the waiters, and they immediately circled the table and filled the diners' glasses with champagne, presumably for a toast.

It was odd that he had waited to make it until now, when dinner was almost over. Cassandra had already drunk one glass of wine, so she would only pretend to drink from this one. Last night's scene with Christopher had brought the evils of excess drinking home to her more graphically than any sermon could.

"I have an announcement to make," the earl said, "and I can think of no more appropriate time than tonight, when my wife and I celebrate thirty-five years of marriage with our closest friends. Please raise your glasses and welcome, with me, Miss Cassandra Davies to our family as my son's future bride."

Cassandra's smile froze as a flurry of excited giggles burst out. The closest gentlemen called out their congratulations to Lord Whitby, who accepted them with every appearance of pleasure.

This was not a surprise to him, she realized. He *knew* his father was going to do this. It probably had not occurred to either of them that she would be foolish enough to refuse. No. It was meant to be a delightful surprise to her. Lady Mayville, she saw, was clapping her hands in ecstatic pleasure, no doubt already planning the wedding.

By her side, Lord Adderly scowled and gave Cassandra a look of pure fury. Cassandra realized that he assumed she had been a party to this in order to force his hand.

He didn't simply look furious, he looked . . . hurt.

Cassandra, feeling terrible, gave him a look of apology. After all his care of her, he had every right to expect more consideration from his ward. Indeed, she *never* would have played him such a trick!

When Lord Whitby took Cassandra's hand and placed a tender kiss on it, Cassandra barely could restrain herself from wresting it away from him. The other ladies practically swooned at the romantic gesture. Lord Whitby looked unpardonably pleased with himself.

"How could you," she whispered, "without a word to me?"

His smile didn't waver.

"I am sorry, my dear," he said smoothly. "I had informed my father of my intentions, and he obviously thought I already had declared myself to your guardian. But there is no harm done."

No harm done! *No harm done!*

In the eyes of society, she was as good as betrothed to Lord Whitby!

"I must . . . go home," she said brokenly.

If she didn't, she was likely to pour the contents of the soup tureen over Lord Whitby's arrogant head.

Cassandra stood, and, bless them, Lady Mayville and Lord Adderly came at once to flank her. She took her guardian's arm in a show of sudden frailty. It wasn't entirely a pretense—she was so upset that her knees were shaking.

"I am . . . not well," she said to an astounded Lord Whitby.

She sounded exactly like the kind of female she most despised—a shrinking violet who succumbed to the vapors at the slightest encouragement.

But she had to leave. Immediately.

"My dear, whatever is the matter?" asked the countess, imperfectly masking her annoyance in a show of concern.

"It is merely the excitement, Mother," Lord Whitby said smugly, just as if he knew everything there was to know about her. He took one of Cassandra's hands in both of his and kissed her brow.

In front of his parents' guests! As if he already owned her!

She was so furious she could not trust herself to speak.

Only her guardian's tight grip on her arm kept her from making a spectacle of herself that the *ton* would not soon forget.

"Come along, missy," he said under his breath in a tone that promised an argument to end all arguments.

Well, he would get none from her. She smiled at him, glad for once that she could count on him to overrule what everyone no doubt thought was her dearest wish.

"I will call on you tomorrow," said Lord Whitby to Cassandra. Amazingly, the smug smile on his face had wavered not a jot.

"We'll see about that, you young puppy," Lord Adderly said in a stern undervoice as he continued to grip his unsatisfactory ward's arm and prepared to march her out to the carriage with Lady Mayville following and murmuring composed apologies to the other guests' expressions of concern.

"What did he say?" the countess asked, looking bewildered.

"Nothing, nothing at all," Lady Mayville said hastily. "We must get Cassandra home. The excitement is too much for the dear little lamb."

Dear little lamb.

Oh, the depths to which Cassandra had sunk!

"You thought you could force my hand, did you, my girl?" Lord Adderly said furiously when they were all seated in the carriage and Lady Mayville had felt Cassandra's forehead, certain she was suffering from some sort of fever since she did not fall like a ripe plum into Lord Whitby's waiting arms.

"No . . . I—"

"Jasper, let the girl alone," Lady Mayville said sternly. "Can you not see she is quite overset?"

"Is she?" he replied. "This is nothing compared to

how overset she is going to be when *I* get through with her! If that young cockerel has the gall to present himself to me tomorrow, I shall send him about his business at once, I promise you!"

Cassandra leaned back against the squabs and closed her eyes in relief.

She was counting on it.

Fourteen

Christopher had spent a sleepless night dreaming of Cassandra.

The way she looked.

The way she smelled.

The way she had kissed him as if he were the most desirable man in the world.

Imagine Cassandra making him feel so alive.

He would have laughed if he weren't so pathetic.

You were drunk, idiot. Very, very drunk, he reminded himself.

The way Cassandra had melted in his arms and returned his kisses with a fire equal to his own had been a mere drunken delusion.

It was why he and all the other misbegotten sots drank the stuff, after all.

He had intended to lose himself in drink again last night because he knew that Cassandra was attending a party at Lord Whitby's house, and the fellow was filling her ears with extravagant compliments.

He had told her she looked like a day-old pastry.

It wasn't hard to guess which of them was going to win her heart.

Imagine, feeling this way about *Cassandra*! He couldn't get over it.

They had to talk.

After only one glass of liquor, he found he had quite lost his taste for the stuff and went to bed early. He wanted a clear head when he talked to Cassandra again.

He was taking no chances that he would make a spectacle of himself by threatening to vomit all over the poor girl when he made his declaration to her.

He did know how to cut a dashing figure, he thought with cruel self-loathing.

Christopher shaved and dressed with special care the next day.

He wasn't the Adonis that Whitby was, but he did know that *some* ladies did not despise his looks.

Of course, he *could* speak to his grandfather first, but he ruled that out immediately. Yes, Lord Adderly would be eager to grant his permission for his heir to pay his addresses to Cassandra, but she would probably spit in his eye and no one could blame her. He would avoid at all costs the appearance of being in collusion with her guardian to force her hand.

No. He would simply tell Cassandra the truth—that he could not live without her—and hope she did not laugh in his face.

Christopher had laughed in the teeth of the worst punishments his captors could give him as a hostage in France. He had risked death over and over in order to escape. He had endured unspeakable conditions in the stubborn determination to survive.

But nothing had filled him with so much terror as the prospect of living without her.

He arrived at Lady Mayville's town house so early that the dew was still on the grass, only to find Lord Whitby just leaving.

The young man looked discomposed, and he gave Christopher a look that should have felled him where he stood.

"'Morning, Whitby," Christopher said guardedly. "What are you doing here so early?"

"Good morning," the gentleman said curtly. "I have just been with your grandfather."

Christopher was properly taken aback.

"You mean . . . you have made an offer for her? Already?"

He was too late. Too late!

Whitby gave him a smug smile.

"Well, the old gentleman cut up stiff over it and refused me outright at first, but he said he would give me a final answer later today after he talks to Miss Davies. I think we both know what *her* answer will be, don't we? So yes. You may be the first to congratulate me."

"Of course," Christopher said woodenly. "Congratulations."

If his felicitations lacked conviction, Whitby was not the man to notice it.

"Thank you," Whitby said as he passed by with a jaunty step to his carriage. He turned back, as if at an afterthought.

"You might put in a word for us with your grandfather," he said. "I know you don't like me or the girl, but I trust you will do the decent thing. She was overcome with happiness when I asked her to marry me. I wish you could have seen her face. So there is no doubt about *her* wishes in the matter."

He had seen her already. He had been accepted.

If he went inside and found his grandfather had capitulated, Christopher would have to smile and pretend to be glad for her. He would have to kiss her on the cheek and wish her happy.

He didn't think he could do it.

But when he turned around to go back to his lodgings, the door opened and a distressed-looking Cassie appeared.

"Oh, it's you," she said, taken aback. Her eyes darted past him. "I was hoping to catch Lord Whitby."

"Sorry. He has already left," he said. He took a deep breath and tried to look cheerful. "So, I am to wish you happy."

"It seems not," she said with a brave smile. "Lord Adderly has made up his mind to refuse his suit."

Christopher put a consoling arm around her and felt like a hypocrite for enjoying it so much. After all, the poor girl was in love with another man. He could not bear to see her look so tense.

"What? Admitting defeat, are we?" he said in a rallying tone. "How strangely unlike you, Cassandra."

Cassandra gave herself up to the comfort of his embrace.

How ironic that her childhood nemesis was the only one who understood this about her. It was a relief that *someone* didn't think she was silly enough to dissolve into a little pool of gratification simply because Lord Whitby had expressed a wish to marry her.

Cassandra bit her lip in frustration.

Christopher was so handsome that she couldn't believe she had been too stupid to see it at once. Had she really declared to her guardian that she wouldn't marry him if he were the only man on earth? Had she told Christopher that she hated him only two days ago?

She still tingled at the memory of his kisses. At the feel of his arms around her.

At the scent of that Mrs. Benningham's perfume clinging to his person. She couldn't forget *that*, either.

What an idiot she was.

And now he was congratulating her on her prospective marriage to Lord Whitby, a marriage she was determined would not take place. He was probably relieved that he needn't fear Lord Adderly would make *him* marry her.

Christopher had kissed her with such passion only two days ago, and now he was wishing her happy with another man.

Cassandra obviously had made a very grave error in thinking he had some feeling for her, but while this was a disappointment, she would not compound it by marrying Lord Whitby. Thank heaven she could count on Lord Adderly to refuse his consent.

She was beginning to realize that stubborn guardians had their uses.

It was unfortunate that she could not catch Lord Whitby to tell him that she did not wish to marry him and thus save him the embarrassment of coming back tomorrow to receive Lord Adderly's formal refusal. She could hardly tell Christopher the truth, however.

He might think his kisses had meant too much to her, and that she could not endure.

Let him believe with the rest of the world that stubborn Lord Adderly had found Lord Whitby's suit unacceptable. She could hardly embarrass a gentleman whose attentions she had encouraged by telling anyone—*especially* Christopher—that she had grown to find his conceit offensive.

How Christopher would laugh at her for her fickleness. She would have to admit he was *right*. And he might guess that she had fallen in love with him, even though she had made a solemn pact with him not to let Lord Adderly force him to marry her.

She would rather die than betray his trust. And her own heart.

"I will put in a word for you and Whitby with my grandfather," he promised. His eyes were solemn.

She looked at him, startled.

"You would do that?" she asked.

"Certainly," he said. He touched her hair and she closed her eyes at the sweetness of it. "I have not always been your friend, Cassandra, but please believe I only want your happiness."

Her happiness.

To marry Whitby, he meant.

Christopher was just like everyone else, after all.

"What made you change your mind?" she asked, trying to hide the hurt from him. "Two days ago, you told me that I would be miserable married to Whitby. I believe the reason had something to do with my sharp tongue and independent nature."

"I didn't mean it," he said apologetically. "I was drunk. I know that is no excuse for saying such things, and I apologize."

"Are you going to apologize for kissing me, too?" she asked.

He looked her straight in the eye.

"No," he said.

He put his hands on her shoulders.

"Cassie, I—"

She caught her breath in anticipation.

He was going to kiss her again! She just knew it!

Then the doorbell rang and Christopher released her and stepped back quickly as the maid came into the hall to answer it.

The maid murmured something to a delivery boy and turned around with Lord Adderly's morning newspaper in her hands. She bobbed a curtsy to them as she passed them to return to the main body of the house.

The spell was broken. Christopher and Cassandra smiled self-consciously at one another.

Before they could say a word, though, they heard an enraged howl from outside the hall and Lord Adderly stalked in, thumping the newspaper with one hand.

"Did you know about this, missy?" he demanded of Cassandra. "Did you?"

She could only gape at him.

"Look at this," he said, thumping the newspaper as Christopher looked over his shoulder to see what had caused him to explode with such fury. "The little chit forced my hand, she and that insolent young pup between her!"

Christopher felt his face pale.

There, at a prominent place on the social pages, was an announcement of the forthcoming marriage of Miss Cassandra Davies of Devonshire to Edmund, Lord Whitby.

Wordlessly, he took the newspaper from his grandfather's hand and passed it to Cassandra.

For a moment she could not breathe.

"Damn it, girl! Have you no shame!" Lord Adderly shouted at her. "I should have known you would play off a trick like this to force my hand! I'm ashamed of you, girl. I didn't rear you to be a conniving little cheat!"

Cassandra felt her lower lip quiver. She couldn't control it. He was *ashamed* of her. He thought sending the announcement to the papers had been *her* idea! It hurt so much to have him think her capable of such a deceitful act that she burst into tears. No maidenly, crystalline sobs, these, but great, racking sobs of despair.

"Please—" she began, but she found it impossible to say anything more. She reached out for Christopher's hand, and he grasped it strongly.

"It's all right, Cassie," he said as he took her into his

arms for a brief hug. "Everything will be all right, I promise you."

She clung to him a moment, but he gently pried her fingers from the lapels of his coat and gave them a comforting pat.

"I promise you," he repeated.

Lord Adderly stalked forward and shook his finger right in her face. Her eyes had been too full of tears to see his approach, so she gave a small shriek of pure nerves.

"I am not going to be blackmailed by you and that whey-faced twaddle-poop, missy!" Lord Adderly shouted right in her face.

"That's *enough*!" Christopher snapped.

His voice was not nearly as loud as his grandfather's, but it cut like the lash of a whip. Lord Adderly closed his mouth and stepped back at once.

Christopher could not bear the pleading look in Cassandra's eyes.

She was counting on him to make this right for her.

And he would, even if it broke his heart in the process.

He would do *anything* to ensure her happiness, even though it meant he could never have her.

What a hell of a time to discover that he loved her that much.

"Headstrong little chit has no idea *what* she wants!" Lord Adderly fumed as Christopher tried in vain to make him see reason.

He should have known *that* would be a lost cause!

Still, he owed it to Cassandra to try.

She had never asked for his help in anything before. He would not fail her now, even though the thought of that mincing man-milliner Whitby touching her made Christopher want to put his fist through the wall.

"Have you ever known Cassandra not to know what she wants?" Christopher said with a snort of mirthless laughter. "She's been telling us what she wants next since she was seven years old."

Lord Adderly gave a long sigh.

"Remember how sad she was? How tiny and frail?"

Christopher remembered the birdlike little creature well. She had just lost her father, and Lord Adderly and Christopher were worried sick because the child refused to eat. She was certain her father would be back any moment to fetch her.

They had been afraid she would die of sorrow.

But there was steel in that little spine, and when she realized her father would not be coming back, her anger made her strong.

Indeed, as an orphan himself, Christopher knew how she felt, although he knew better than to tell *her* that more than once!

"He'll be good to her," Christopher said, although the words stuck in his throat.

"He'll let her rule the roost, you mean," Lord Adderly said scornfully.

"Can you imagine any arrangement that would suit her better?"

"No, you've got that right, boy!"

"So you'll give your consent?" Christopher prompted.

"I suppose I have no choice now that it's been puffed off in the papers. I wouldn't be surprised if the headstrong little minx drafted the announcement herself."

"You can't call Cassie a minx," Christopher said

sternly. "A minx wheedles and manipulates her victims into giving her what she wants by using her feminine wiles. Cassie goes after what she wants with a club."

It occurred to Christopher that encouraging Whitby to send a premature announcement of his impending marriage to Cassandra was not her style. She was more inclined to take to the mat with her grandfather and fight it out, toe to toe.

This only proved how desperate she was to marry the fellow.

Lord Adderly gave Christopher a straight look.

"It sounds almost as if you admire her."

"I do admire her," he said softly. "There is no one like her."

"She needs a strong man to control her, but she won't find him in Whitby."

Lord Adderly regarded his grandson with an accusing stare.

"*You* could have done the job if you had exerted yourself in the least. You're a handsome fellow. The ladies like you. But you had to chase that widow!" He said "widow" as if it were a dirty word.

"At any rate," Christopher said, "Cassandra has made her choice."

"You think I should give in with good grace," Lord Adderly said with a sigh. "I suppose you are right, much as it angers me to give in to blackmail. There isn't a prettier word for it."

"You're only disappointed because I won't have her lands to march with ours and enhance the consequence of our legacy," Christopher pointed out.

"Is that what you think?" Lord Adderly looked shocked. "You think the only reason I wanted you to marry her was to have her fortune and lands to add to the estate?"

"Isn't it?"

The old man actually looked hurt.

"I'm a selfish old man," he admitted. "I wanted to keep both of you with me."

Christopher's mouth dropped open.

"I deserve your skepticism," Lord Adderly said. "I have not always been the most affectionate of grandfathers. Or the most indulgent of guardians."

An understatement, Christopher thought.

"But I . . . care for you." Lord Adderly couldn't look his heir in the eye when he made this embarrassing admission. "I'm proud of both of you."

"You . . . are?"

"I'm a lonely old man," he said bitterly. "I lost my wife, my son, and my daughter-in-law. They were my whole life. Then I had only you. Can you begin to understand what that was like?"

"They were my whole life, too," Christopher said softly. "I think I do. I used to think you hated me. Nothing I did ever pleased you. When you did not pay a ransom to have me released from France, I naturally thought you did not care."

Lord Adderly hung his head.

"I deserve that. I should have investigated further. I have failed you. I have failed you both."

"No," Christopher said. "You have never failed me. It was not *your* fault that I was taken hostage."

"I insisted that you go on the grand tour with your tutor."

Christopher gave a short laugh.

"Don't berate yourself over that. I couldn't wait to see the world outside Devonshire, and you know it!"

"When I learned you were taken hostage, I made inquiries immediately. When I was informed of your death, it was like losing your father all over again. But

I still had Cassandra. After that, I couldn't bear to let her out of my sight."

"So you refused to give her a London Season until now, even though her fortune and birth entitled her to it. Instead you kept her in Devonshire and tried to marry her off to one of the local men so you could still keep her near. Did you ever tell her why? Did you tell her you love her and couldn't bear to part with her?" He gave a long sigh. "Of course you didn't," he said, answering his own question.

Lord Adderly looked defensive.

"She would have thought I was a doting old fool, and despised me for it."

Christopher shook his head.

"Well, if you love her, you will let her marry Whitby."

The old man pursed his lips as if he tasted something sour.

"I have no choice when you put it that way," he said. "There! Are you happy now?"

"Yes," Christopher lied. Never was a victory so bitter. "You'd better end the poor girl's suspense and tell her she can marry the fellow after all."

"You tell her," Lord Adderly said. His shoulders were slumped in defeat. "I can't look at her right now."

"Me!" *He* did not want to see the rapture on her face when she learned that she would be able to marry Whitby.

"I can't. Not now," Lord Adderly said, looking like a broken old man for the first time in Christopher's memory. "I'm tired. I'm going to my room to rest."

Never had Christopher known his grandfather to need rest in the middle of the day. He was an old man, now, and Christopher hadn't even noticed.

"Of course," Christopher said. He was worried about him. "Get some sleep."

He braced himself.

"I'll tell her."

He found Cassandra in the parlor. She had a basket of needlework beside her, but she wasn't working on the pretty pattern of embroidery. She was nervously wringing her hands in her lap.

She sprang to her feet and walked toward him.

"Christopher?" she said anxiously.

He forced a smile to his lips.

"It's all right, Cassie," he said, taking both her hands in his. "He has consented to your marriage. Congratulations."

Her mouth fell open in shock.

"No," she whispered. "I don't believe it."

"Believe it," Christopher said bracingly. Did she have so little faith in him? She looked as if she might cry again.

"But he said nothing would convince him to consent."

"I managed to convince him, but only barely," he said. "Truly, he does have your best interests at heart."

"Oh, Christopher!" she cried, and before he knew what she was about, she threw herself into his arms. She was crying. He could tell from the way her shoulders shook.

He closed his eyes and patted her on the back.

Was there ever such sweet anguish? Holding Cassandra in his arms while she wept for sheer happiness that she was going to marry another man was killing him.

Lady Mayville swept into the room just then.

"My darling!" she cried. "I have just heard your wonderful news! Jasper is as grumpy as an old bear, but he *has* consented. Where will we go first?"

"Go?" Cassandra sniffed. "I don't know what you mean."

"To shop for bride clothes, of course!" The elder lady's eyes were sparkling. "I know there has not been time to set a date for the wedding, but it is *never* too early to shop for one's bride clothes. Such a triumph, Cassandra. I am so proud of you!"

Cassandra's lips were white. She was still in shock, Christopher supposed, at her good fortune. Who would have thought she would go all vaporish?

He patted her on the back in a brotherly fashion. Brotherly. That was all he could be to her now.

"I must go," he said, because he couldn't stand to be here when Whitby returned and received the good news. "I have an appointment."

"At your nasty old Gentleman Jackson's, I'll wager," Lady Mayville said indulgently. "Run along, then, Christopher, for we *are* to talk of bride clothes, and I know of no subject *that* is more boring to you men."

He bowed, careful to avert his face from them for fear that they might see the emotions he tried to hide.

"Christopher!" called Cassandra before he was all the way to the door. She ran after him, and he reluctantly turned to meet her.

She had her hands together, as if in prayer. He placed his on each side of them.

"I . . . I must tell you," she said brokenly as she raised her tear-streaked face to his. "You must know—"

"I know," he interrupted her. He was in no mood to listen to her ardent expressions of gratitude. "You don't have to thank me."

He raised their joined hands to his lips and kissed the tips of her fingers.

He forced himself to smile when he wanted to weep right along with her.

"I have stood as a brother to you since you were a grubby little brat," he said. "Please believe I would do anything to ensure your happiness."

A brother.

A lie of this magnitude should have made his tongue turn black and rot off.

"I must go," he said again, and made his escape.

Fifteen

The next week was a nightmarish whirl of activity for Cassandra.

Lord Whitby had been suitably gratified when Lord Adderly formally gave his consent to the marriage, but Cassandra could tell he had been in no doubt of the outcome of his suit, not really.

It was all Cassandra could do to support the character of a happy bride. She did not know how to look when the countess complimented her on her dignified demeanor at one of the prenuptial parties.

"I have no patience with these flighty young girls who behave like giddy little ninnyhammers at such a time," Cassandra's future mother-in-law said. "It is of great satisfaction to me that my son need never blush for your manners."

"Thank you, my lady," Cassandra said, although she deeply resented the countess's patronizing attitude.

Cassandra was trying her best to pretend to be delighted about her marriage, but apparently she was not successful if the bridegroom's mother was complimenting her on her restraint!

Lord Whitby himself appeared to be in no doubt of her feelings.

She did not know how she would bear his kisses

now. His sly references to their wedding night filled her with trepidation.

Thank heavens Lady Mayville insisted that it would take her at least a year to plan a suitable wedding when Whitby pressed for the marriage to take place at the end of the summer.

She must tell him.

Somehow, she must tell him.

This soon proved to be an impossible task, for even though the world acknowledged they were to be husband and wife, they were never alone.

When they went driving in the park, Whitby's carriage was thronged with well-wishers. At balls, all of Whitby's and the earl's connections were eager to do their duty by dancing with Whitby's fiancée. And when he came to call at Lady Mayville's house, the parlor was always full of other visitors.

It seemed all the world loved a happy bride.

And if she was only pretending to be happy—if she only toyed with her food and her laughter was more nervous than mirthful—no one seemed to notice.

Well, almost no one.

One day Christopher came to the house in answer to his grandfather's summons. Lord Adderly declared the young jackanapes could bloody well leave off his riotous raking about town long enough to pay his remaining family a proper visit.

So, while Cassandra sat trapped in the parlor with a bevy of young ladies exclaiming over Lady Mayville's enthusiastic description of the bridal gown being designed by Miss Lacey, Christopher sat sipping tea and watching her closely.

What he observed was that Cassandra's smiles didn't reach her eyes, and that her thoughts seemed preoccupied. Whitby was expected. She kept watching the door.

This was exactly why he had avoided the house. He couldn't bear seeing Cassandra ecstatic about marrying another man. Especially if that man outwardly was a pattern card of perfection.

Whitby, he felt quite sure, had more finesse than to get drunk, force himself on the poor girl, then get sick to his stomach and have to spend the night on the parlor sofa. Christopher had crowned this masterly performance by revealing one of his most closely guarded secrets—he was afraid of the dark and had been since he was taken hostage.

Cassandra had reacted without horror to his behavior, but then she was prepared for such deviations from him.

Hadn't he been half dressed and chewing on a spinach leaf when she discovered him in the garden, unshaven and gaping at her like a lunatic? And, because she had said the same of him first, hadn't he declared that she was the last woman on earth he wished to marry, even though, to his dazzled eyes, she looked like an angel come to earth with her halo of golden hair shining in the morning sunlight?

No wonder she had fallen into Whitby's arms like a ripe plum.

His eyes narrowed, though, when Cassandra jumped at the sound of the bell. She took a deep breath as if steeling herself to face an ordeal.

When Whitby came into the room to bow over Cassandra's hand and she smiled up into his face, Christopher realized he had just been imagining things.

All the ladies had been struck to silence when he came in.

"You have such charming company that you will not wish to go driving with me today, after all," Whitby said. The ladies all tittered. Lord Adderly scowled.

"Come along, Christopher," the impatient Lord Adderly said to his heir. "We have listened long enough to all this talk of furbelows."

Christopher could hardly bring himself to tear his eyes away from Cassandra's face.

Something *was* wrong. But Cassandra's next words persuaded him that he had been mistaken.

"I would love to go driving with you," Cassandra said. She sounded relieved. "I am certain our guests will excuse me."

Sly titters all around.

Naturally the young lovers couldn't wait to be alone, even if they would be surrounded by other people in carriages and on horseback in the park.

Cassandra seemed willing enough—even eager—to go with him.

It could be, Christopher decided, that all the attention she was garnering from well-wishers—all the parties and wedding preparations and constant scrutiny—was making her nervous.

He could understand that. Perfectly.

It did not mean that she was regretting her engagement.

That was merely wishful thinking on his part.

Still—

He followed her out of the room when she excused herself from Whitby to get her pelisse and hat.

"Is everything all right, Cassandra?" he asked when he caught her arm and she turned to face him.

He hadn't been imagining it. Her eyes were all nerves before she averted her face from him.

"I do not know what you mean," she said.

Cassandra had jumped nervously when she felt his hand on her arm.

"Cassandra," he said earnestly, "if something is wrong, you must tell me. You know I will do everything I can to help you. Is it my grandfather? Has he been pestering you? Or has Whitby—"

His voice trailed off, inviting her to tell him why she was behaving more like a frightened rabbit than an ecstatic bride.

It was tempting, so tempting, to throw herself into his strong arms and sob out her dilemma—that she had been trapped into marrying one of the most handsome and eligible bachelors in London. How pathetic that would sound. And how unfair to Whitby.

She owed it to Whitby to tell him face-to-face that she could not marry him. Now, before the wedding preparations went any farther.

But Whitby had been obliged to go into the country on some matter of estate business with his father right after the announcement had appeared in the newspapers, and even when he returned, she hadn't had a moment alone with him.

She would tell him. Today. On the way back from the park.

And she would not insult him by having him learn it from someone else, even though Christopher seemed willing to fight her battles for her.

That would be cowardly.

Besides, she hated the thought of admitting to him that she had decided she didn't want to marry Whitby after all. He would think her fickle.

If she told Whitby first, he could release a dignified statement to the newspapers saying they had decided they would not suit. Neither he nor she would have to say anything more to anyone.

"Cassandra?" Christopher said, sounding concerned. "You are trembling, poor girl. Tell me what is wrong. Is it the fact that my grandfather and Lady Mayville won't hear of your wedding taking place sooner than a year from now?"

"I do not know what you mean, Mr. Warrender," she said, looking him in the eye. She felt her face flame with embarrassment.

"That's it, isn't it," he said. His voice had gone deadly. "You want the wedding to take place sooner because—" He grasped her shoulders and gave her a little shake. "Has he . . . did you . . . Are you with child, Cassandra?"

"With child!" she squeaked. "How dare you suggest such a thing to me?"

"If you are, I'll kill him," he said in that same deadly voice.

"No, no! You are mistaken, Christopher. Truly."

He released her.

The red haze of anger cleared from his vision.

She was distressed, but there was no mistaking the conviction in her voice.

Again, he had made a complete fool of himself.

"You must forgive me," he said, trying to salvage his pride. "I have stood as a brother to you for all these years." He smiled. "Not a good brother, I'll grant you, but the least I could do is defend your honor if it became necessary."

"Happily," she said, "that is not the case."

"No, I can see that. If you wish, I can talk to my grandfather and see if he will agree to move the wedding up. No wonder you are nervous. I would be, too, if I had to look forward to a year of this wedding business."

"You are a great deal too busy, Mr. Warrender," she

said with some asperity. "I do not need *you* to meddle in my affairs."

Christopher felt his anger rise.

His intentions had been good, and here she was throwing them back into his face.

"Well, pardon me for trying to help."

"I don't need your help," she snapped.

They were standing face-to-face, he glaring down at her and she with her hands on her hips, looking like a little wet hen. She was so adorable, Christopher wanted to kiss her.

He could imagine how she would react to that!

Since he had no wish to wear the angry imprint of her hand on his face all day, he scowled at her instead.

"I wish Whitby joy of you, you little shrew!" he said.

At that moment, Whitby himself stepped into the hall.

"And he accepts, gladly," he said with a humorous little bow in their direction. "Run along, darling, and fetch your bonnet. The park awaits."

Cassandra bit her lip and went off immediately. Christopher gave a snort of annoyance.

She certainly did not obey anyone else so readily.

He was a fool, and Cassandra was absolutely right. He had no business interfering in her affairs.

"You and Cassandra cannot be in the same room for more than a moment without quarreling, can you?" Whitby observed pleasantly.

"It has always been that way between us."

"So she has said."

"Has she?" Christopher frowned, annoyed that Cassandra and Whitby had been talking about him together.

Had she told him he was afraid of the dark?

"Of course," Whitby said complacently. "Cassandra tells me everything. Our minds and hearts are as one."

Christopher gave a snort of contempt.

If he had to listen to much more of this, he *would* draw the fellow's claret!

Mercifully for the state of Whitby's heretofore unbroken nose, Lord Adderly stomped into the hall.

"Christopher!" he snapped. "I haven't all day. Come with me, if you please. There are matters we must discuss."

"At once, sir," Christopher said immediately.

"Lord Whitby, there is something I must say to you, and it will not be easy," Cassandra said in the first moment they had alone. From the time they entered the park, their carriage had been mobbed with well-wishers.

But then one of the earl's oldest friends tipped his hat to them, and Whitby and the old gentlemen embarked upon a conversation about politics.

"A man needs to be married," the old gentleman said with a friendly nod at Cassandra. "Pretty little thing, too."

"Thank you," Whitby said smugly, as if he had anything whatsoever to do with it. Cassandra was getting very tired of being treated as if she were deaf and mute in the company of Whitby and his male acquaintances.

All the more reason to say what she must say and make an end to it.

When the old gentleman moved on, she recklessly took the plunge.

"Edmund, I cannot marry you," she cried. Her

voice was at least an octave higher than usual. "I am sorry for it, but I simply cannot."

Good heavens! This was not the tactful, well-rehearsed speech she had meant to deliver.

Incredibly, he smiled at her. He guided the carriage to the side and took both her hands in his.

"What is this, my love?" he asked, but before she could answer, he added, "Bridal nerves, I am persuaded. Perfectly natural, I assure you."

"No, I—"

"You must allow me to be the judge of what is best for you," he said complacently. "You are worn to a thread with all the parties."

"No, I am not. I—"

"Tut, tut, dear. Of course you are. I'll tell you what it is. A year is too long to wait. I shall tell Lord Adderly again that he must move the wedding up. We can be married in August. Won't that be better, my pretty?"

August! Oh, sweet heaven!

"No, no!" she objected. "You must believe me. We would not suit!"

He gave a long sigh.

"I know what it is. I frightened you with my ardor, but I promise you I will not do anything you do not like. We will live as brother and sister after our marriage until you are ready."

Ready?

Cassandra shuddered. She would *never* be ready. Not two months from now. Not a year from now. Not *ten* years from now.

She felt like more of a villainess than ever, allowing matters to proceed so far.

"Lady Mayville will be frantic. We could not possibly be married so soon," she said. "I have not even had a fitting for my wedding gown yet."

What was she saying? She was *not* going to marry this man.

"We could be married tomorrow, if you only say the word," he said, lowering his voice to an insinuating whisper. "We could elope to Gretna Green."

"Never," she said vehemently. "Never would I do such a thing!"

"Think about it. All this folderol over the wedding would be over, and you would be mine. We would go into the country, away from town, where you may be comfortable."

Into the country? Was he *mad*?

The last thing Cassandra wanted to do was go into the country where people discussed nothing but crops and the weather, where all the provincial parties had the same few families at them, where life was so dull there was no bearing it.

Cassandra was getting sick and tired of everyone assuming she was a high-strung ninny with bridal nerves.

"I know my own mind," she told him furiously.

"I know you do, darling," he said sweetly. Then he turned from her, took the reins, and moved the carriage back on the road. "You are worn out," he said. "I will take you home."

"You do not understand," she protested. "I am *not* going to marry you."

"Of course you are," he said, smiling and nodding his head as other park occupants called greetings to him and Cassandra. "Your grandfather has given his consent. The announcement has appeared in the newspapers. I refuse to listen to another word of this foolishness. After a short rest, you will feel more yourself."

Finally, after talking herself blue in the face, Cassandra lapsed into depressed silence.

Listlessly, she watched Whitby smile and accept the well-wishes of others, just as if she had never spoken a word.

Elope with him! Never!

She had tried to do the decent thing and tell him first, but now she had no choice.

She would go to Lord Adderly and beg him to tell Lord Whitby she did not wish to marry him, even though she would have to swallow her pride and admit she had made a terrible mistake.

But when she returned to the house, determined to see her guardian at once, she found that both he and Christopher had departed for Devonshire on an urgent matter of estate business and would not return for a fortnight.

"Lady Mayville, I am at wit's end," she sobbed after she had burst into tears and her guardian's concerned sister had made her sit down on the sofa and pressed her vinaigrette upon her.

Mercifully, there was no company in the house when she learned that her guardian was gone from the house because she behaved like a hysterical ninny.

"I know what it is," Lady Mayville said comfortingly. "It is mere bridal nerves, love. Perfectly normal."

"Did it happen to you, ma'am?" Cassandra asked. "Did you go into your betrothal feeling that if you had to go through with the marriage, you would go mad?"

Lady Mayville blinked.

"Actually, no," she admitted. "But that is nothing to say to the matter. Perhaps I was wrong to insist that we need a year to plan the wedding—"

"No, no!" Cassandra cried. "I am not going to elope!"

Lady Mayville gasped.

"Elope! Who said anything about that?"

"Whitby," Cassandra admitted. "Today he pressed me to elope. He said we could be married tomorrow if I would say the word. I did not know what to do. He was so insistent—"

"Ah, I know what it is. How I shall give that young man a piece of my mind when I see him," Lady Mayville said, certain that she had discovered the mystery. "That impetuous boy! He has frightened you with his advances. You cannot expect a man in love to regard the prospect of waiting a year for his wedding night with anything but impatience, but Whitby should not have suggested an elopement. It would give a very *off* appearance, unless . . ."

She broke off and regarded Cassandra with narrowed eyes.

"Dearest," she said carefully as she took Cassandra's hand, "is there something you are not telling me? Has Whitby . . . are you . . . ?"

Oh, good heavens!

"Absolutely not!" Cassandra snapped. "How can you think me so dead to propriety as to . . . do what you are suggesting?"

Lady Mayville gave a relieved sigh.

"Well, then," she said complacently. "There is no harm done. Go to your room and rest now, my dear, until dinner. I promise you, you will feel much better."

Knowing that she had thoroughly botched the matter, Cassandra went to her room, threw herself upon the embroidered satin counterpane, and burst into tears of abject misery.

Sixteen

Christopher returned to London grubby, dusty, and in no mood for his own company, so after shaving, dressing in his town clothes, and having a meal at his club, he decided to pay a visit to Caroline Benningham.

It was early enough in the evening that if she had no previous engagement, perhaps they might see a play. Or go to a concert.

Anywhere there was noise and people, so he wouldn't have to be alone with his own depressing thoughts. The manor in Devonshire was an empty shell without Cassandra's presence. At every turning, he and his grandfather expected to see her.

The thought of her married to Whitby depressed Christopher as the dismal conditions and disgusting food of Bitche never had, for when he was in France he had had hope.

Now he had none.

Cassandra was lost to him. Forever.

How was it possible to mourn so bitterly something he truly never had?

Well, his friend Caroline would cheer him up.

Her attitude toward life and love was so cynical that he had no fear that she would insult his sensibilities by waxing poetic about Whitby and Cassandra's approaching nuptials. The betrothal had been the talk of their neighbors in Devonshire who had, of course, read the announcement in the London newspaper.

This was so uncomfortable that he and Lord Adderly had concluded their business with the land steward as soon as possible so they could return to London.

Christopher forced a smile to his face when he was admitted to Mrs. Benningham's house. No use in alarming the butler with his lugubrious countenance.

"Is Mrs. Benningham in?" he asked politely.

"Mrs. Benningham is occupied at present," the butler said with a distant smile.

Of course.

He had been gone a fortnight. Mrs. Benningham would not spend the time waiting for him to come back. She had found a new escort. Why would she not? *He* had certainly been less than satisfactory in that regard.

"I see. Well, if I may leave my card—"

At that moment, a man clad in black stepped into the hall and gasped when he came face-to-face with Christopher. He was still pulling his coat together, and his hair was in some disorder.

"Whitby," Christopher said, frowning.

"'Evening, Warrender," the fellow said, brazening it out. "I did not know you were back in town."

Christopher didn't speak. He couldn't.

The fellow was seeing Mrs. Benningham behind Cassandra's back!

"So it appears," he said when he found his voice.

"Come, come, man," Whitby said. "There is no reason to make such a piece of work of it. Do stop by the club, and we'll talk."

"Be sure we will," Christopher promised.

"Christopher!" cried Mrs. Benningham as she

tripped into the hall. She, too, looked as if she had dressed hastily. "How delightful to see you. Do come in."

"I think not," he said dryly.

"Go, Edmund," she said to Whitby, and the man did so.

Before Christopher could follow, Mrs. Benningham grasped his arm.

"No! You must get control of your temper first, or you will do something you regret," she said.

He took a deep breath.

"Caroline—"

"Not here," she told him, and towed him away.

"We are going into the parlor," she told her butler. "We are not to be disturbed under any circumstances."

"Very good, madam," said the butler.

"You knew he was betrothed to Cassandra," Christopher said angrily to Caroline.

She blushed crimson.

"You must believe that if he was in love with her, or she with him, I would not have brought him here," she assured him. "But as theirs is to be a marriage of convenience—"

"A marriage of convenience! Did he tell you that?"

"Well, of course," she said, surprised. "He told me she shrinks from his touch, and that she merely wants the title and position he will bring to her. And he merely wants her fortune."

"What utter nonsense."

"The girl is frigid, Christopher. Edmund said so."

"*Edmund*, is it?" he said furiously. "I'll kill him."

"You're jealous," she said ruefully. "I wish I could think it was because of me, but it isn't, is it?"

"No, my dear. I'm afraid not," he said. "I must go."

"You aren't really going to kill him, are you?" she

asked anxiously. "It wasn't entirely his fault. We met quite by chance earlier today, and one thing led to another, and—"

"Please," he said, closing his eyes. "Spare me the details."

"Christopher, I beg of you—"

"I won't kill him," he said, "but you can be damned sure I am going to have an explanation for why he has betrayed her before the ring is even on her finger."

"It is not in man's nature to be faithful," Caroline said bitterly. "Your little Miss Davies would have learned this soon after her marriage, if not before."

"Farewell, Caroline," he said impatiently. "I must go."

With that, he shook off her clinging hands and made his way to his club, where Whitby was seated at a table, drinking gin.

"Come to challenge me to grass before breakfast for replacing you in the divine Caroline's affections, have you?" he said jovially enough.

The bloody fool thought he was so angry because of *Caroline*.

"Caroline can defend her own honor," Christopher said.

"Decent of you," Whitby said, nodding. "It was a bad moment when I met you at her house. You had a look on your face that was enough to curl my liver."

"What were you doing there?" Christopher asked. "As if I don't know."

"What of it?" Whitby asked with raised eyebrows. "A man has needs, and that frigid little chit I am pledged to marry is certainly not woman enough to satisfy them."

Frigid? Cassie?

He thought Whitby had merely told Caroline this

to get between her sheets, but he could see now the fellow believed it.

"Did you . . ." The red haze clouded Christopher's vision again, just as it had when he suspected that Whitby had anticipated his wedding vows by making love to Cassandra and getting her with child.

"God, no! She didn't give me the chance. She shrank from me as if I were the devil incarnate. It was plain she had never had a man's tongue in her mouth before. Nearly gagged."

"Did she, now?" Christopher said, feeling better despite his frustration.

He could have told Whitby that her reaction to *his* kisses had been far different, but he had no wish to get off the subject at hand.

"Then why did you offer for her? And why have you been plaguing my grandfather to give his permission to move the wedding up to this summer? When we were in Devonshire, he received two letters from you on the subject."

"The stubborn chit won't agree to elope, that's why! Oh, you were right about her," he said bitterly. "Stubborn as bedamned! Most women would swoon at the thought of being romantically swept away to Scotland, but not *she!* Oh, no. *She* must have her elaborate wedding at St. Paul's."

"Well, every girl wants a nice wedding, Whitby," Christopher said. "Why do you care? You obviously are managing to keep yourself entertained, if what I witnessed tonight is any indication."

"Ah, the delectable Mrs. Benningham," Whitby said with a sigh. "What a cozy armful *she* is. Unfortunately, though, I can't wait a year to marry Cassandra unless she'd like to be married from Fleet Street Prison."

"In debt, are you?" Christopher said as enlightenment dawned at last.

"Up to my neck," Whitby said with ironic cheer. "And this time my father refuses to pay the nonsense. Oh, he settled my debts of honor right enough. But the tradesmen are dunning us both to death, and he told me it was time I found a young lady of fortune to marry and settled my bills myself."

"So you thought Cassandra easy pickings," Christopher said glumly.

"Of course. Well-dowered, well-favored. Pretty little thing, fresh from the country. Easily impressed at first. I had her hanging on my every word, and then something went wrong. Oh, you were right about her. At first I thought you wanted the girl's dot for yourself." He gave a snort of derision. "Then she revealed her true nature."

"I wonder that you will not break it off and move on. It is not as if you lack for females eager for your attention."

Whitby missed the sarcasm entirely.

"My father and mother have consented to this marriage," he said bitterly. "If it doesn't come to fruition, the scandal will be disastrous to me. My father will *not* pay my debts, and my creditors will close in. When it becomes known that I must marry a fortune, do you think the matchmaking mamas will not lock up their daughters? I will have to look among the daughters of the Cits to save my bacon."

"It won't be the first time a gentleman has repaired his fortunes by doing so," Christopher pointed out.

"Give me credit for *some* pride, Warrender," Whitby said. "No, Cassandra and I will rub along quite comfortably together once she learns her place."

"Her place," Christopher repeated.

"Once we are married, I will install her at my estate and resume my life in London."

"She won't like that," Christopher said, remembering how much Cassandra disliked the prospect of making her home permanently in the country.

"She will have nothing to say to the matter once we are married. What do you care, anyway, Warrender? You don't even like the girl."

"Shut up, Whitby," he growled as his fingers curled into claws. He so badly wanted to wrap them around the blackguard's throat and squeeze until his tongue turned black.

"I know what it is," the other man said. "You are angry with me for taking your place in Mrs. Benningham's bed. Well, if you are going to leave town for a fortnight, you can't expect a woman like that to sit tamely at home waiting for you to return."

"You are such a cloth head, Whitby," Christopher said, stomping to the door.

He knew Whitby was wearing a smug smile, certain that he knew exactly why Christopher was so angry.

Let him.

He wouldn't be smiling once he went to Lady Mayville's house and demanded that Lord Adderly call off the wedding.

"I don't give a bloody damn in hell that Lord Adderly has retired for the night," Christopher roared when Lady Mayville's butler tried to deny him the house. "Wake him up!"

Wide-eyed, Cassandra and Lady Mayville ran into the hall.

"Christopher! Whatever is the matter?" Lady Mayville exclaimed.

"Are you drunk again?" Cassandra asked baldly. Her hair was halfway down her back, as if she had already begun preparations for bed. Frigid. Hah! Cassandra had more passion in her little finger than Whitby had in his whole . . . well, the fellow was a bumbling idiot. Whitby had his *tongue* in her mouth, the devil take him! Christopher had half a mind to turn around, go back to the club and pound Whitby into powder.

Cassandra's warm hand grasped his.

"Here, come in and sit down before you rouse the whole neighborhood," she said. "You had better not let Lord Adderly see you in this condition."

"I am not drunk," he said a bit more temperately. "I need to speak with my grandfather. At once."

"You just spent a fortnight in the country with him," Lady Mayville pointed out. "Can you not wait until morning?"

"No. This is urgent."

Cassandra's brow wrinkled as she considered him.

"Why are you looking at me like that?"

Because I am about to break your heart.

"Cassandra, please believe I have only your best interests at heart," he said earnestly.

"All right," she said with a touch of her old humor. "Now I *am* alarmed."

God, how he loved her.

"What is the meaning of all this racket?" demanded Lord Adderly as he entered the room, looking irrationally dignified in his nightshirt and cap.

"Sir!" Christopher said in relief. "I must speak to you at once!"

Lord Adderly's shrewd eyes searched Christopher's face for a moment.

"Come along, then. We'll use the library," he said as he led the way out of the room.

"I wonder what *that* was about," Lady Mayville said when the men were gone.

"I have no idea," Cassandra said, "but we can hardly go off to bed after that."

Lady Mayville seated herself on the sofa.

"Ring for tea, my dear," she said. "We may as well be comfortable. I do hope it is nothing horrid. You do not think Christopher has got himself into debt or some hussy with child, do you?"

Cassandra's lips thinned as a picture of the lovely Mrs. Benningham leapt into her mind.

"I am sure I do not know," Cassandra said as she pulled the bell.

"I suppose all we can do is wait," Lady Mayville said with a sigh. "Such is a woman's lot in life."

"The way Christopher looked at me," Cassandra said. "As if he felt sorry for me. It is most puzzling."

Lady Mayville's eyes widened and she raised one trembling hand to her throat.

"You do not think it is Whitby, do you? That something terrible has happened to him?"

Cassandra despised herself for the way her heart leapt at the notion.

If something terrible happened to Whitby, perhaps she would not be expected to marry him.

She had not had the opportunity, yet, to broach the matter of breaking off her betrothal to her guardian because she and Lady Mayville were at a musicale when the old gentleman returned to the town house and went at once to bed.

He was completely exhausted by the journey, the butler had reported, and he had left orders that he was not to be disturbed under any circumstances.

Cassandra, frustrated, had no choice but to wait until morning to broach the matter.

Perhaps if Christopher's business did not put Lord Adderly into too foul a temper, she could talk to him when Christopher had gone away again.

When the maid answered the bell, she ordered tea and coffee, because Christopher, she knew, preferred that beverage, and settled down with Lady Mayville to wait.

Seventeen

"You were right," Christopher said without preamble when Lord Adderly was seated in the library.

Christopher was too agitated to sit down, so he paced back and forth in front of the fireplace.

Lord Adderly gave him a look of surprise.

"Perhaps this was worth being awakened from a sound sleep," he said sardonically. "I do not believe you have said those words to me once in your entire life. What was I right about?"

"Cassandra's marriage to Lord Whitby. It must be called off at once."

Lord Adderly scowled at him.

"I never wanted to allow it," he said. "*You* were the one who insisted the chit must have her way."

"I was wrong."

"You were wrong," Lord Adderly repeated. "I must be dreaming."

"I'm *serious*," Christopher said. "The fellow only wants her for her fortune. He is badly dipped, and his father has refused to pay his debts. So he plans to marry Cassandra and keep her confined in the country while he spends her fortune."

"The devil you say!" he said. "I thought the fellow was head over heels in love with her. He keeps badgering us to move the wedding up, but Belle won't hear of it."

"He has been trying to convince Cassandra to elope in order to keep the constables from carting him off to Fleet Street Prison," Christopher said. "He admitted as much to me. I encountered him when he was leaving Mrs. Benningham's house in a hurry with his clothes hanging half off him. Naturally, I demanded to know why he was paying clandestine visits to Mrs. Benningham when he is supposed to be in love with Cassandra."

"Oh, ho! Now I know why you are in a passion," Lord Adderly said sagely.

Christopher scowled at him.

"He may have Mrs. Benningham with my goodwill," he said, "although I had thought better of the lady's taste. But I will not permit him to deceive Cassandra. She doesn't deserve it."

"No, by God," Lord Adderly said.

He went to the door, opened it, and bellowed into the hall.

"Cassandra! Get in here, girl!"

"Grandfather," Christopher said in alarm. "This is a matter of some delicacy. The girl is in love with him. You have to be gentle—"

"Gentle! I'll give you gentle," Lord Adderly scoffed. "Cassandra!"

"Here, my lord," she said, wide-eyed. Lady Mayville was right behind her.

"You may as well hear this too, Belle," Lord Adderly said, indicating that the two ladies were to be seated.

While they regarded him from the sofa, he stalked over to Cassandra and put his finger right in her face.

"The wedding is off, as of this minute!" he shouted. "Don't give me any argument. That is my final word on the matter."

Cassandra's mouth dropped open. Poor girl.

Christopher walked over to the sofa and put one hand on her shoulder to give it a gentle squeeze.

"Courage, my girl," he said softly. "I am as sorry as I can be, but there is no help for it. You cannot marry him."

"But—" she began, clearly at a loss.

"Jasper, how dare you!" cried Lady Mayville. "How dare you break Cassandra's heart!"

"Belle, this is none of your business," Jasper said. "This is all your fault for putting romantic ideas in her head about the young jackanapes."

"But Cassandra is to have a fitting with Miss Lacey for her bridal gown tomorrow," Lady Mayville protested. "The church has already been reserved. And we are to have a ball in honor of the couple on—"

"Well, cancel it! Cancel all of it," Lord Adderly demanded. "I have no doubt that Lacey woman will still send me a bill."

"But why?" Cassandra asked in disbelief.

"He's after your fortune, missy," Lord Adderly said almost gleefully. "He doesn't care for you at all. Didn't I tell you so? Didn't I? He admitted as much to Christopher."

She turned her shocked blue eyes on Christopher.

"Is this true?" she asked almost calmly.

He sat next to her and took her hand.

"Yes, Cassandra," he said gently. "I am afraid so. He has been begging you to elope with him because he is in dire straits. It was marry an heiress or go to Fleet Street Prison."

"I see," she said, looking down at their joined hands. "You must think me the biggest fool in Creation."

"No. Never," he said.

"Caught the fellow leaving Mrs. Benningham's house half dressed," Adderly declared.

"Grandfather," Christopher said reproachfully. He put his arm around Cassandra's shoulders. "If you had not kept Cassandra secluded in Devonshire all this time, she would have recognized an oily-tongued rascal when she encountered one."

"So, it's *my* fault, is it?" Lord Adderly said. "What about you? *You* were the one who insisted she should be allowed to marry the fellow. Well, that just beats the Dutch." He shook his finger again at Cassandra. "We're going back to Devonshire tomorrow," he told her, "and you're going to marry Christopher. I've had enough of London for one lifetime."

"Grandfather!" Christopher exclaimed.

"I have spoken!" Lord Adderly said. He gave his tearful sister a compelling look and propelled her from the room. "The two of you can just make your minds up to it."

With that parting shot, he slammed the door behind him, and Cassandra and Christopher could hear his loud, almost gleeful shouts ordering the servants to prepare for his and Cassandra's departure for the country.

Christopher tightened his arm around Cassandra, but she pushed him away and stood.

"You must think me a complete fool," she said, bowing her head. Her face was hidden from him by the golden curtain of her hair.

"No. Never," he said, appalled. "I could cheerfully have shot Whitby for using you so." She looked up at that, and he gave her a teasing look. "What do you say, Cassandra? It isn't too late."

A burble of slightly hysterical laughter burst from her lips.

"Don't tempt me," she said ruefully.

"That's my girl," Christopher said, pleased that she

no longer seemed in danger of turning into a watering pot. "*He* is the fool. You deserve a better man, one who will appreciate you."

"Yes," she said with a sigh. "However, the chances of my finding this paragon now are limited since I will soon find myself back in Devonshire."

"Ah, Cassandra, I am so sorry," Christopher said. "I begged my grandfather to break the news to you gently."

He took her in his arms.

"I swear to you," he said earnestly, "that in time you will forget him."

"I think," she said, staring up into his eyes, "that I have forgotten him already."

Because he could resist her no longer, Christopher bent and kissed her. His hands tangled in her soft, shiny hair, and the delicate strands clung to his fingers. He could taste the salt of her tears on his lips.

"No," she said huskily as she broke off the kiss and turned away from him. "You're only kissing me because you feel sorry for me. Well, I don't need your pity."

"I do feel sorry for you," he said, "but I also think you are the most beautiful, desirable woman in the world."

Cassandra gave him a skeptical look.

"Since when?" she asked.

He thought about it for a moment.

"I think that day on the terrace in Devonshire when you gave me your breakfast and defended me against Grandfather's raving," he said. "You were so sweet to me. You treated me like a beloved idiot child."

"I was *not* sweet to you. As I recall, I told you I would never marry you. Not if you were the last man on earth."

"True. But I didn't blame you. You looked like an angel, all bathed in sunlight."

Her lips spread in a tremulous smile.

"An angel. How absurd. You had better not let your grandfather hear you talking such nonsense. He'll have the banns proclaimed before the cat can lick her ear, and then you will be sorry."

"No, Cassandra," he said deliberately. "I would not be sorry. I would consider myself the luckiest man in the world."

"*Don't*, Christopher. I know you mean to be kind, but—" She broke off and took a deep breath. "It's going to be so horrid. I will have to tell Whitby, and he will be so angry, and another announcement will be placed in the newspapers, and everyone will be whispering behind my back."

He tipped her chin up with one finger.

"Do you know what is going to be even more horrid?" he asked ruefully.

Mesmerized, she shook her head slightly.

"Admitting to my grandfather that he was right all along, and listening to him cackle with glee when I ask him for permission to pay my addresses to you."

"You are not joking? You want to marry me?" she asked in disbelief. "Truly?"

"Truly. You don't have to answer now. I know it is too soon—"

At that she gave a shriek of delight and threw her arms around his neck. Unprepared, he lost his balance and sent them both thudding into the sofa. It creaked backward a few inches and slammed into the wall.

"*This* is my answer!" she cried as she placed ardent little kisses on his cheek.

"But—"

"What has happened?" cried Lady Mayville as she ran into the room with her brother at her heels.

She came to an abrupt halt at the spectacle of Christopher half reclining on the sofa with Cassandra sprawled on top of him.

"Christopher has just asked me to marry him," Cassandra said sunnily.

"Is this true?" Lord Adderly asked. A smile was already overspreading his face.

Christopher raised himself to a seated position and settled Cassandra into the crook of his arm.

"Absolutely true," he said lovingly. He couldn't seem to take his eyes off her. "I would very much like to marry this delightful little baggage. If you please, Grandfather. Although I do hope you and Aunt Belle will not make me wait a whole year for her like you tried to do with Whitby."

"Autumn is a beautiful season," Cassandra suggested eagerly to her aunt. "Can we not be married in autumn? It does not have to be a very *large* wedding."

"Oh, my darlings!" cried Lady Mayville before her brother could reply. "How wonderful! Thank heavens I haven't had time to cancel Cassandra's appointment with Miss Lacey for the bridal gown fitting."

Even this did not have the power to spoil Lord Adderly's triumph.

"I was right all along," Lord Adderly said, grinning from ear to ear. "I knew this would be a perfect match. Did I not say so, Belle? Well, I cannot be dawdling here. I must draft an announcement for the newspapers."

At that, he turned and left the room with Lady Mayville close on his heels.

Christopher rolled his eyes, and Cassandra gave a soft laugh.

"You're right," she teased. "That *was* rather horrid."

"Jasper," they heard Lady Mayville exclaim, "it would be exceedingly gauche for you to send the announcement of Cassandra's betrothal to Christopher to the newspapers, when the announcement of her broken betrothal to Lord Whitby has not yet appeared. *He* has not even been informed yet. You should wait at least a month—"

"Women! Always eager to spoil a fellow's fun," Lord Adderly complained loudly. "I'll give Whitby the bad news myself. It will be a pleasure. I never did like the fellow."

Cassandra's smile faded, but Christopher kissed her frown away. He knew exactly what she was thinking.

"Let Grandfather do it. He'll enjoy it so much, and, besides, Whitby deserves it, darling," he told her.

"But I owe it to him to tell him myself—"

"You owe him nothing. Besides, you don't have time for idle chitchat with your former suitors," he said as he bent to kiss her again. "I intend to keep you very, very busy until autumn."

Eighteen

Caroline Benningham gave a sigh of long-suffering.

"There goes another one," she said to her escort at Cassandra and Christopher Warrender's wedding breakfast. Lady Mayville's town house was filled with light and laughter. "Yet another bachelor snapped up by a dewy young ingenue. It is to weep."

The wedding at St. Paul's had been lovely. And Christopher had given Caroline such a glowing smile on his way down the aisle lined in yellow and russet flowers with his radiant and expensively gowned bride on his arm that Caroline was actually glad she came. Especially since her smart new bishop's blue ensemble had arrived from Miss Lacey's only the day before.

Lord Whitby gave an identical sigh.

"They look happy."

"They *are* happy," Caroline said resolutely. "And *I* am happy for them."

"Of course you are," he said sourly and he raised a glass of wine to his lips.

"None of that," she chided him with a bright, artificial smile on her face. "Smile. That's why we are here. To save face by pretending we have nothing but good wishes for the bride and her new husband. It was rather civilized of them to invite us. Now all the gossips will see us toasting the newly wedded couple for all the world as if we weren't both still smarting from being dropped like a pair of burnt crumpets."

She waved to Lady Mayville, who beamed at her.

"Well, I do wish them the best," Lord Whitby admitted. "Especially since my father has agreed to pay my debts after all because he feels so much sympathy for what he imagines is my great disappointment. I should have known he was only bluffing about letting me go to Fleet Street Prison. So there is no urgent need for me to marry, after all."

He bent his handsome golden head closer so he was whispering seductively into Caroline's delicate, pearl-adorned ear.

"I thought that later we might share an intimate supper at the Piazza, and perhaps afterward—"

Without looking at him, she raised her hand and spread it against his face to push him away as if he had been an overaffectionate lapdog.

"I hardly think so," she said sweetly. "I asked you to escort me to the wedding for appearances only. It will be some time before you are in my good graces again. *Don't* forget it. Smile. Here they come."

At that moment, the bride and groom approached their table. They both were so radiant that Caroline really *was* happy for them. Christopher winked at her.

"I hope you are enjoying yourselves," Cassandra said. "We are so delighted you could attend our wedding."

She actually seemed to mean it, Caroline thought, but why shouldn't the little minx be overflowing with the milk of kindness?

Another member of Caroline's court dead and married before his time.

Pitiful. Absolutely pitiful.

Lord Whitby, though, took the bride's hand and kissed it.

He looked into her face with such a wistful expression of what-might-have-been that Caroline nearly applauded. If he found himself in dun territory again, he could easily recoup his fortune on the stage.

"I wish you very, very happy, Cassandra," he whispered. "Indeed, I do."

"She will be," Christopher said as he snatched his bride's hand away from him. He lowered his voice. "No thanks to you."

Whitby gave Christopher an audacious little salute as he ushered his bride away.

The newlyweds passed a grinning Lord Adderly, who raised his glass in a toast to them as they walked by. At his side was Lady Houghton. The lady winked at them.

"You don't think—" Christopher said with an indication of his head in their direction.

"They were sweethearts when they were young," Cassandra said. "And I would not be surprised. She has been widowed for several years." She gave a happy sigh. "Such a nice party."

"Would you like to stay longer?"

Cassandra laughed.

"Not on your life!"

Christopher gave her hand a squeeze and accepted his hat from a footman. Then he helped Cassandra into a beautiful ermine cloak. Once outside, he signaled a groom to bring the flower-bedecked curricle drawn by matched chestnut horses forward. It was his wedding present to her.

He boosted her into the driver's seat and she took the reins in her gloved hands. Christopher leapt into the seat beside her.

Christopher jauntily waved his hat in the air. Cassandra blew kisses.

And they were off.

Discover the Romances of
Hannah Howell

Thrilling Romance from
Lisa Jackson

Call toll free **1-888-345-BOOK** to order by phone or use this coupon to order by mail.

Name_____

Address_____

City_____ State _____ Zip _____

Please send me the books I have checked above.

I am enclosing $_____

Plus postage and handling* $_____

Sales tax (in New York and Tennessee) $_____

Total amount enclosed $_____

*Add $2.50 for the first book and $.50 for each additional book.

Send check or money order (no cash or CODs) to:

Kensington Publishing Corp., 850 Third Avenue, New York, NY 10022

Prices and Numbers subject to change without notice. All orders subject to availability.

Check out our website at **www.kensingtonbooks.com**.

DO YOU HAVE THE HOHL COLLECTION?

More Zebra Regency Romances